ASTI SPUMANTE

CODE

A Parody

THE
ASTI SPUMANTE
CODE

A Parody

TOBY CLEMENTS

TIME WARNER
BOOKS

TIME WARNER BOOKS

First published in Great Britain as a paperback original in April 2005
by Time Warner Books

Copyright © Toby Clements 2005

The moral right of the author has been asserted.

A CIP catalogue record for this book
is available from the British Library.

ISBN 0 7515 3768 3

Typeset in Perpetua by M Rules
Printed and bound in Great Britain
by Clays Ltd, St Ives plc

Time Warner Books
An imprint of
Time Warner Book Group UK
Brettenham House
Lancaster Place
London WC2E 7EN

www.twbg.co.uk

THE
ASTI SPUMANTE
CODE

A Parody

CHAPTER ONE

The first bullet missed its target, but the trajectory of the 9mm-jacketed missile – from the end of the silenced SIG Sauer P228 pistol, past the nose of the seated curator and across the vault of the Grand Gallery of the Grand Bibliothèque, Brussels, through three separate oaken shelves, each time coring out a worm-hole of priceless vellum, until it found its final resting place in the spine of an ancient folio of *The Epic of Gilgamesh* – alerted Monsieur Gordon Sanitaire to the danger he now faced.

Sanitaire turned to the shadowy figure in the doorway, silhouetted against the harsh light of the entrance lobby, and he knew at once with a flash of dazzling clarity that the man had come to kill him.

'So,' he said, his voice suddenly hoarse with adrenalin, 'you have found me.'

It was not a question. It was a statement of fact.

The figure at the door merely grunted.

'I knew you would eventually,' Sanitaire continued. 'But if you think I can help you, my friend, you are mistaken.'

'Too much talk,' the figure growled, his red eyes glowing. 'Tell me where it is.'

'Never!'

The single word was followed by another spit of fire from the muzzle of the gun. This time the bullet caught the curator in the shoulder, spinning him off his chair and throwing him across the floor. He came up against some bookshelves with a sickening thud. A heavy tome fell from the top shelf. Sanitaire stuck his hand out and caught it. It was a first edition of Chaucer's *Canterbury Tales*, he could not help noticing, valuable beyond belief.

The figure at the door had not moved. 'Tell me,' he demanded again.

'I cannot,' gasped Sanitaire, his eyes clenched in pain.

'Don't play games with me, you old fool. The others are all dead.'

'And so you come to me.'

There was another shot. This time the bullet flicked Sanitaire's right ear. Blood poured down his cheek. The curator calculated. Three bullets. The SIG, Swiss-made, he knew, had a clip of nineteen bullets. How many extremities could he afford to lose before the man at the door ran out of ammunition?

His only chance was to set off the alarm. But how? If only he could . . . He picked up the Chaucer again. It was weighty, with a gold clasp across the embossed vellum jacket. His fingers traced the pattern: a Celtic knot, similar to one he had seen in Perigord that time with Emily, before they had had their . . . disagreement, when they were visiting the castles of the Knights Templar.

'What?' his attacker demanded.

Sanitaire had been thinking aloud. Now he needed to act. With the very last reserves of his strength he drew back his arm and hurled the book at the famous Rose Window – the famous one above the famous door, carved from a famous single piece of rosewood – to the library's famous Lazarus Wing. How apt, Sanitaire thought, reflecting on the story of the dead man being brought back to life. He decided not to share his thoughts with the figure at the door. The book sailed end over end through a beam of pink-stained light and broke through a small pane at the bottom-right corner of the window. Five o'clock. Vespers. A beam of light from the spot-lights outside speared through the darkened library, falling on a high shelf near the famed painted ceiling. Only one man in the world would understand the mean-ing of that now.

The alarm sounded. A deafening buzz like the rotors of a distant helicopter. A Chinook, perhaps, or a Gazelle.

CHAPTER TWO

Something had disturbed the sleep of James Crack. He woke in a panic. The phone was ringing by the bed, an unfamiliar – eerily European single tone repeated – *brrrr brrrr* over and over again. In the first few moments of consciousness, all Crack could think was: where the hell am I?

He looked around. He found himself lying between linen sheets, under a duvet? 'Jeez,' he muttered. A duvet. Whatever next. At the foot of the bed – a four-poster, he noted, and made in mahogany, ah, and now whatever did that mean? – he, or someone known to him anyhow, had left, or draped rather, a John Lewis dressing gown. A John Lewis dressing gown? Things were spiralling out of control. He shook his head. And at that moment he saw on the pocket, emblazoned in neat stitch, the legend 'Holiday Inn, Brussels'. That took care of where he was, but now who was he? Luckily, next to the insistently shrill telephone he discovered a name-tag: Professor James Crack.

It all came back to him now. He was James Crack, Professor of Para-literal Meta-symbolist Studies at the University of Catt Butt, Nebraska, and recently voted seventeenth most intriguing person by *Bugle* magazine, which had caused his friends and colleagues great merriment.

But what was he doing in Brussels of all places? Fortunately, underneath the name-tag, he found a flyer: 'An Evening with Professor James Crack'. He had been invited by the Vrije Universiteit Brussel, or some other university, to read from his latest book, *Below the Surface: The Hidden Meaning of Superficial Stuff*, and to give a guest lecture on the meaning of meaning. The evening had gone well, he recalled – standing room only, himself oblivious to the attentions of the young women in the audience – but now he was tired. Tired, tired, tired.

And all that remained to do was to remind himself what he looked like. Thank God! A mirror. Full-length, startlingly near his bed. His hair, still full and thick, was on end, and his eyes – usually unusually blue and so clear that they reminded some women, usually, of sapphires at the bottom of a mountain stream – were now hazy.

'You need a vacation, James,' he said to himself. And he meant it.

It had been quite an evening, but now here he was, lying in bed at twelve-thirty in the morning. He had been asleep for just an hour.

He snatched at the Louis XVI phone, still ringing at his elbow.

'Yes. What is it?' he demanded.

'*Pardon*, Monsieur Crack. *C'est le concierge ici. Bonsoir. Je suis vraiment desolé, vous comprenez, mais il y a quelq'un ici qui demande*—'

'Let me stop you right there, mister. Do you realise the time?'

'*Oui*, monsieur, *mais*—'

'Listen, pal. It is gone midnight, I just flew in from Chicago, Illinois, and I am on the floor with jet lag.'

'But, monsieur, it is only five-thirty in the evening in Chicago.'

'It is?'

'*Oui*, monsieur, and besides, this person is very . . . 'ow you say? Important.'

Crack sighed. It was obviously going to be one of those nights. He had become something of an unwilling celebrity since being appointed the youngest professor at the University of Catt Butt, Nebraska, but it had been his last but one book, *Signs and Symbols Easily Discernible in Everyday Objects*, published the year before and a surprise Christmas bestseller, that had really brought the lunatics out of the woodwork. No doubt this was some crackpot who had followed him home, eager to correct some typo or other.

Crack groaned. 'Look, I'm sorry. Just have them leave

their name and number and tell them I'll call them back in the morning.'

'But Monsieur Crack, they are already on their way—'

The man was cut off by three thunderous crashes of a fist against Crack's hotel room door.

'Professor Crack?' came a voice from the far side, baritone and profound. 'I am Lieutenant Jacques Dijon of the Toutes Directions Bureau de la Cage aux Folles, Bruxelles. I wish to 'ave a word with you.'

Crack paused. The TDBCFB was the Belgian equivalent of the FBI. He crossed the room, his bare feet luxuriating in the carpet's deep pile, and opened the door quickly. The man who faced him was overweight, with small inky eyes and a greasy mop of tousled hair. His clothes – a store-bought, grey-checked jacket, a white onion-skin shirt and light-grey trousers – were tight in the wrong places, and tonight he smelled of frying.

'Yes,' said Crack. 'What is it?'

'Professor Crack—'

'Please,' Crack interrupted, 'just call me Monsieur Crack.'

'OK, Monsieur Crack. I wish you to come with me. Capitaine Taureau, my boss, would like your assistance on an urgent matter.'

'Can't it wait?'

'I used the word "urgent" for a purpose, monsieur. I assumed you would have understood its significance.'

Crack raised his eyebrows. Oh God, he thought. One of them. Ever since his surprise bestselling book *The Significance of Words and Some of Their Meanings* had been translated into thirty-seven different foreign languages, Crack was occasionally pulled up on intricate, bizarre and obscure linguistic technicalities. The man went on.

''Ave a look at this photograph, will you, Monsieur Crack? I took it myself an hour ago, with a 4.8-mega-pixel digital camera finished in brushed stainless steel.'

'Nice,' murmured Crack.

'Thank you. I am saving up for the 6-mega-pixel version, but you know, on a lieutenant's salary . . .' Dijon shrugged and did not bother to finish the sentence. 'Anyhow, monsieur. Do you recognise this man?'

'He is dead?'

'*Oui*, monsieur. As a dodo.'

A dodo? Now where did that come from, the professorial part of Crack's brain wondered. He peered at the photo. It was a six-by-nine glossy. A close-up of a man who appeared to be knee-deep in snow. He was wearing what looked like a fur coat, and seemed, from the angle of his limbs, which were contorted into unnatural and ghastly positions, as if he had been in some kind of severe road traffic accident, except that there were what looked like train tracks in the back ground. A train crash? There was something wrong about the photo, but at first glance, Crack could not say exactly what it was. He began fighting a stealing sense of unease. Why was he being shown a photo of a dead man by a police officer at twelve-thirty in the morning?

'No,' he answered after a pause. 'No. I don't know him.'

'Hmph.'

The lieutenant put the photo back in his hip pocket. Crack noticed the man had the smallest feet imaginable, and wore dainty, pointed black dancing slippers, topped off with a tiny silver snaffle.

'Do you know,' Dijon continued, 'or rather, did you know, a man named Gordon Sanitaire? He is, or was, the curator at the Grand Bibliothèque, here in Bruxelles.'

Alarm bells began to ring. 'Sanitaire? Why, yes. I was supposed to meet with him this evening after my lecture. He never appeared. I assumed he—'

'You assumed what, monsieur?'

'That he had been delayed and could not make it.'

'That is all?'

'Yes.'

'Hmm,' Dijon mused, chewing a damp, cuddish lower lip. 'And you did not attempt to contact him?'

'I did not. To tell you the truth, I was grateful for an early night.'

Dijon raised himself on tiptoe and attempted to peer into the hotel room past Crack's perfectly lean six foot two frame.

'You are with someone, perhaps?'

'Lieutenant. If that is all?'

'Regretfully not, Monsieur Crack. I must ask you to accompany me to the famous library, where Capitaine,' again Dijon pronounced the word 'cap-i-taine' as if it were some foreign word, 'Taureau is waiting to meet you.'

'But—' Crack began, knowing it was useless.

'Come. We will take my car.'

CHAPTER THREE

Brussels is a small city, even by Belgian standards, and it had not taken Stoat long to walk from the Grand (or big) Bibliothèque to Rue Jeanne. Stoat was an immensely powerful, but short-legged and left-handed man with a thick pelt of hair – some even called it fur, although not to his face – that curled out from under his shirt-sleeves and collar, and even from below the hems of his dark trousers. This 'fur' changed colour with the season – white in the winter, a sandy shade of brown in the summer, which had given rise to his nickname: Stoat, or the Stoat, or Mr Stoat. No one knew his real name. That had been lost in the mists of time, when he was recruited from behind a till at a well-known London bookstore aged just thirty-six. It was something he did not talk about. He now travelled on two passports, one for winter and one for summer, so as to not have to explain the colour change at every border control.

Rue Jeanne was a smart street of tall redbrick buildings interspersed between large apartment blocks in a wealthy part of the city and there, using his key – a long tube of brass with a series of jagged crenellations at one end and a flat circular disc, stamped with a hole, at the other – Stoat entered number seven. It was an imposing residence that had once been a high-class brothel. It had since been bought and put to the services of quite another pastime. It was now the home of the English Book Guild, Brussels, and at any one time, in any one of its ten bedrooms, any one of the Guild's many thousands of members might be staying on business.

Many thought the Guild a sinister organisation, but it was registered at Companies House in London and its presence in Belgium had been officially sanctioned by none other than King Albert I (1908–83). The Guild was dedicated to the apparently harmless pursuit of encouraging people to read, but as with any organisation the world over, there were extreme elements within its membership. There were also schisms among those who piloted its course through the choppy waters of international literature, and the media had somehow got hold of the idea that a group of some of the most powerful publishers on earth had gained an influence within the Guild's ranks, and were seeking to apply the organisation's vast resources to their own ends. This group, known simply as the Uxbridge Road

Group, after their sinister meeting place in London, were now the most active wing of the Guild, and though their methods of recruitment were controversial, they had persuaded more people to read books than many thought possible. More than two million in paperback at the last count.

Stoat quietly placed his book bag, with the SIG Sauer inside, on a marble side table, and crossed the marble-floored hall to the double doors that led through to the kitchen. It was deserted. A pot with a lid stood on the cooker. Some kind of rice dish. He dipped a spoon in and ate hungrily.

'The Lord has provided food,' he muttered. 'And purpose to my life.'

When he had finished Stoat carefully wiped his mouth and fingers and began to clean the SIG Sauer, disassembling it and wiping the mechanism down with oblongs of cotton waste primed with a synthetic oil. Stoat did not relish taking human life, but he had come to understand that the enemies of the Uxbridge Road Group were ruthless and bent on its destruction. He knew with a cast-iron certainty that they must be destroyed, that fire must be fought with fire. It was not, after all, the first time that the URG had had to defend itself.

When the SIG was cleaned, reloaded and stored in its velvet-lined box, Stoat picked up the telephone and dialled a number.

'It is done?' growled a voice at the other end before the first ring was out.

'Yes, Brown Owl, it is done.'

For reasons of security, the URG had adopted these quaint titles in the 1920s. Again, some saw this as sinister, but there was really nothing to it.

'They are dead?'

'All of them.'

'Did they provide the information we seek?'

'Three confirmed the existence of the *Mûre-de-Paume*, the legendary keystone.'

There was a quiet gasp of excitement at the far end of the phone. 'It exists!'

'Yes.'

'But?'

'The Grand Master would not talk.'

'I see. The others?'

'Talked.'

'And?'

'The Central Library of the European Commission.'

'In Brussels? How they tease us. So.'

'So.'

'You must go there tonight. There is no time to be lost.'

'But the Central Library will be closed, Brown Owl, especially at night.'

'Here is what you must do.'

After hearing what Brown Owl had to say, Stoat replaced the telephone in its receiver. It had been a long night, but it was not yet over. He collected his book bag and walked silently to his room, his heavy serge suit rough and chafing against his naked buttocks as he stalked up the sweeping marble stairs, the thin leather suspenders cutting into his bare shoulders. When he found his room he shut the door behind him and double-locked it, sliding a knee-bolt across the aperture and inserting a wedge under the thick planks of the armoured steel. He propped a chair against the handle. Not all the rooms in the house had this sort of security, nor did they have rubber walls. Stoat had known many rooms like it and, as he knelt at the Spartan, heart-shaped bed with a satin-effect flounced valance and began his preparations, he once more gave up a prayer of thanks to the Guild.

'Thank you,' he murmured, shedding his jacket. Then, hooking his thumbs under the brutally thin leather straps of his suspenders, he pulled. These suspenders – sometimes called braces in Europe – were worn by all the URG members to remind themselves that they were not working hard enough. The rough material of Stoat's unlined serge trousers bit deeper into his flesh, cutting him again and again, and reminding him of his purpose in life.

'Only to serve . . . Only to serve . . .'

CHAPTER FOUR

Dijon was a good driver and, with his emergency light flashing and his siren wailing, he forced his dark saloon quickly through the tunnels that seemed to run through Brussels as if stitched into the city's fabric by some giant hand. At Place Quelqueplace Dijon turned a sharp left and the car skidded over a cobbled square, coming to an abrupt halt at the foot of a flight of stairs that led up to the famous Palladian entrance to the Grand Bibliothèque, sharply illuminated this evening by rank after rank of yellow floodlights, as if someone, or something, were expecting an enemy bombing raid. The car's passenger door was opened for Crack before he could even undo his seatbelt, compulsory in Belgium, even if you are sitting in the back seat of the car. Another police officer loomed above him: medium height, with tiny dark eyes in a fat face. His chops were greasy and unshaven, and his untucked shirt hung from below the ill-fitting blue uniform. Tonight he had a mayonnaise stain on his lapel. He looked like a caricature of a modern suburban Belgian.

'Monsieur Crack?' he spat, covering the professor in a wave of garlic-and-wine-flavoured breath. 'Follow me.'

Crack unfolded his impressive perfectly toned six foot two frame from the back of the car and stood for a second, stretching his weary limbs. He had always hated travelling in cars ever since, as a boy, he had made a trip from one town to another.

The Grand Bibliothèque was an extraordinary building, a confection of intersecting right angles, so that each of its four perfectly straight sides met in four perfectly geometrical corners. Built in 1823, many believed it was modelled on the Pentagon, in Washington, the headquarters of the most powerful army the world had ever seen, but this was a mistake. It was in fact based on a far older symbol, the square, which cropped up almost everywhere you cared to look, but was not, in fact, a shape that existed in nature. Crack had seen a plan of the library when he was a student and had been stunned to find that its shape bore a remarkable similarity to that of a book, albeit that much larger, and a bit chubbier.

Crack looked up at the windows. He was startled to see that some of them were illuminated, while others were not. Legend had it that there were 1,472 window panes – exactly the same number of pages in the Penguin Classic edition of *War and Peace* by Leo Tolstoy, a novel about a battle that had been fought not too far from the city the skyline of which the Grand Bibliothèque now dominated. It was an incredible coincidence that 1472 was also the name of the cologne that Crack liked to use whenever he travelled in Europe.

'Monsieur Crack?' the impatient voice demanded from the top of the stairs. ''Zis way.'

Crack decided not to share his thoughts with the police officer and dutifully followed him up the stairs and through the revolving doors. They walked for five minutes through a maze of darkened corridors by which time he felt thoroughly lost.

'Jeez,' he said, 'remind me not to come to this place alone at night without a flashlight.'

'You would not be allowed in, anyway, monsieur,' replied the police officer, humourlessly. 'The doors are locked.'

'It was a joke.'

'I see. But Monsieur Crack, I must warn you that Capitaine Taureau is not one for light-hearted witticisms of that sort.'

'OK, I get the message.'

They walked on in silence until they eventually reached a large atrium, where, in the pale sidelights,

Crack could make out a short, frankly tubby little man, with loose, five-o'clock-shadowed jowls, a large belly that was ill-contained by a greasy leatherette blouson and poorly cut trousers. He was carrying something under his arm – an oblong object made from many different sheets of paper bound together in thick card – and he seemed to be waiting for Crack.

This, he thought, must be Captain Taureau.

'Professor Crack?' the man demanded. His voice was rough from too many cigarettes and shouting at his wife.

'Professor James Crack. Yes. And you are Captain Taureau?'

'Cap-i-taine Taureau, *oui*. I am sorry to have disturbed your sleep, but there is something with which I need your help. Come with me.'

Taureau led Crack to a small goods lift, the sort that is used to move books about a library from the stacks deep in the basement to the reading rooms. The lift provoked no thoughts in Crack's mind whatsoever. When it arrived, he stepped in and stood facing Taureau, his eyes all the time on the object that the police officer held clamped under his arm. It looked to Crack like a book.

'It is a book,' confirmed Taureau. The professor was surprised at such directness. Before he could ask any more questions, the lift jerked to a stop. Taureau threw back the cage and pushed open the outer door. They were now in a brightly lit hallway. Ahead of them Crack could read a sign that pointed the way to the Grand Gallery, but tonight the ornate doorways were blocked by grey sheets of metal.

'Come,' was all Taureau said, and he led Crack around a corner to another entrance. This one was smaller, a side entrance, and only half blocked by the metal shutter, as if it were a guillotine blade that had become stuck on a little screw fastened into the frame of the contraption halfway to its macabre destination. Taureau raised an eyebrow and nodded at the gap.

'*Après toi.*'

Crack hesitated.

'Please, monsieur. It is very important.'

Shrugging, Crack knelt and began crawling under the gap. It was not a feeling he enjoyed and he banged his head on the metal shutter – two sheets of steel, he now noticed, with a filling of some other metal, probably titanium.

'Oh, very cool, James,' he muttered to himself.

Once inside, a scene of such destruction greeted his eyes that he was not at first able to comprehend just how bizarre a sight it was.

The famous Grand Gallery attracted scholars, students, academics and statesmen (political leaders, diplomats and public officials) from all corners of the globe. They came to see the shelving, handmade from

oak planks taken from the legendary Library of
Alexandria, as well as the massive number of books.
There were reputed to be more books in the Grand
Gallery than in any other room in the world. Many of
them were paperbacks, of course, but others were of
immense, incalculable value and some were first edi-
tions, including a folio of the Ten Commandments. As an
associate professor, a younger James Crack had done
some research in this library on his first book, *Connections
and How to Make Them Work for You*, a student text he had
written as part of his doctorate. While he was here, he
had been instrumental in the startling discovery that a
notepad the library had misattributed to Henry
Kissinger – the famous diplomat – had in fact been John
Milton's everyday book.

It was a terrible sight for James Crack, then, as he
surveyed the damage before him. The floor, famous
for its use of wood, was covered as far as the eye could
see in very very finely shredded paper, so that it looked
as if it had been snowing inside all week. The shelves
were festooned with scraps of this same paper lying
three or four inches deep. Through this, though, ran
two lines of books, perched on their sides, so that their
spines stuck up through the 'snow'. These were the
train tracks Crack recognised from the photo that Dijon
had shown him. He began to follow them, his shoes
crunching through the paper. He reached a point where

they seemed to diverge – one set going off into a gap between the shelves, the other twisting towards an arc light. James walked towards the light.

What he saw there made him gasp.

CHAPTER FIVE

Professor James Crack had never met Gordon
Sanitaire, but he had heard great things about the
revered curator. Now here the man was, lying in a pool
of light thrown from the arc lamp, the 'snow' around
him thick with dried blood. He was naked except for
some strange covering of an unidentified material
caking his arms and upper body. It was not the first
impression the revered curator would have wanted to
make, mused Crack.

Sanitaire's right ear was ragged, and his blood-
crusted wounds were dark and ghastly. He lay in a
frightful position, one arm clutching something to his
chest, while the rest of his body was thrown this way
and that, as if it had suffered a hugely traumatic impact.
On the floor in front of the body the snow had been
cleared, however, and a shaky hand had written out
some words and numbers in what looked like dried

blood. Crack bent to study the words. There were three lines:

Blow off the well informed wart hOg smoothie
Pliant criminals canoodle
Tidy Histogram

What in the world did it mean? It was gibberish.

'But who would do this to a man?' muttered Crack.

'Sanitaire did it to 'imself.'

Taureau had followed Crack along the railway lines and stood just outside the pool of light.

''Imself?'

'Yes. 'Imself. We believe he was shot by a person or persons unknown earlier this evening, but Sanitaire managed to set up this . . . this scenario before the gut shot — a notoriously slow and painful way to die, monsieur — finally did for 'im.'

'Jeez.'

'*Exactement*! The killer was trapped outside the gallery when Sanitaire set the alarm off, but by then it was too late.'

'Too late?'

'Too late for us to catch the killer or get in to help *le* curator.'

'How did he set the alarm off?' Crack asked.

'Look.'

Taureau pointed at the famous Rose Window, where the hole in the pink pane at the bottom right let in a beam of light from the floodlights outside. Crack shook his head and looked around him again. It just did not make sense. He stooped to pick up some 'snow'. The strips of paper were all torn by hand. He shivered.

'Is it me or is it cold in here?'

'The window, perhaps, or the illusion of the snow.'

'It must have taken him hours.'

'*Oui*, monsieur, although I believe he was a fast worker.'

'And it took you that long to get to him after the alarm had gone off?'

'Monsieur, this is Belgium. There was paperwork to complete and cigarettes to be smoked and complaints to be made. We got here as soon as we could.'

'But he had time to shred all this paper and—'

Something struck Crack with the force of five tons. What was that coating with which Sanitaire had covered himself? Was it . . .? Could it be . . .? Good God! It was. It was chewed leather. Sanitaire had chewed the leather bindings of the books around him and had fashioned himself a long dark coat. Crack felt his hair stand on end. Why? Why would he have done all this?

'*Ne touchez pas!* Don't touch!' barked Taureau, but Crack simply had to see what it was that Sanitaire hugged to his chest. He grasped the man's right arm and pulled it away, his grip sending up a soggy squirt of spit and ancient leather from the dead man's sleeve. What Crack found there made him gasp again. Could it be? The revered curator was clutching a slim, blue, perfectly bound copy of a book so rare that Crack had only ever seen it behind a bulletproof glass display cabinet in a vault deep in the bowels of the London Library. Crack had believed there were only two existing copies of *Troublesome Engines*, written by a man named Wilbert Vere Awdry, or 'Reverend' Awdry, and illustrated by C. Reginald Dalby. There was the London Library copy and one in the private collection of a Briton named Lord Tod Wadley, a knight of the Order of the *Bassineurs*, an expert in para-literalism and a personal friend of James Crack. And yet here was another copy, unknown until now, grasped in the bloody hook of a dead curator. What could it mean? Was this what the killer was after?

'What is it?' demanded Taureau, angry now.

Crack shook his head. *Why would a man go to such lengths?* he asked himself. *Why would he set up this bizarre scenario? Was he trying to tell them something? Could that be it? Was it a message? Think, Jim, think!*

'This book,' replied Crack, tugging it free of the bloody grasp, 'is incredibly valuable.'

'Let me see.' Taureau took the volume. Crack thought that those hands were probably only the third pair to touch this book in the last twenty years, without special

CHAPTER SIX

James Crack sat down on one of the library's leather chairs. It creaked menacingly. He felt faint. Taureau was still busy with the book, unaware, for the moment, of its para-literal symbologistic import.

'Look,' the captain said. 'Sanitaire 'as written something.'

Perhaps this was the clue they were looking for?

'What is it?'

Taureau started to read the words in his strong Belgian accent. It was clear they were in Italian, a language with which Crack was more than familiar from having spent six years at the Università Degli Studi di Roma, in Italy's Rome. The police officer stopped, embarrassed by his inability to perfectly accent the passages, and he passed the book to Crack.

'Here, you read it. I can't make 'ead nor tail of it.'

What Crack saw startled him. Unease welled up

within him again. The words were laid out in a strange form, the handwriting a crude disguise for the inner meaning of the message:

If this book dares to roam,
box its ears and send it home
to: Hubert Condom, aged 8½
16, The Close
Newport
Gwent
Wales
United Kingdom
Europe
The World
The Universe

Crack had once seen something like it in an ancient scroll in the secret vaults of the Vatican, but never since. The implicit violence made him shudder. *Box its ears? From which kind of primitive culture did that spring?* He could see some slight differences between this and the Vatican text, but he did not want to bore the captain with details. The last lines were clearly an address, probably in Wales. He took a black notepad from a top pocket and jotted the lines down, his handwriting neat, simple, muscular, meaningful.

'What does it mean, Monsieur Crack?'

'It is a code of some sort. I can't be sure what yet. But it refers to something.'

'Is it the sort of thing that Sanitaire might have written to tell us who killed him?'

'I suppose it is possible, but it could have been written a very long time ago.'

'Hmph. What about this?'

Taureau nodded to a nearby desk also covered in the paper snow. Gordon Sanitaire's diary was a large leather-bound planner with brass tags on each corner and the initials GS embossed into the cover's fine grain. Taureau opened it. Although there was some extraneous information on the pages at both the beginning and at the end of the book – time differences, tides, eclipses, distances between the world's major cities and so forth – Crack was startled to see that the meat of the diary was divided into exactly 365 separate sections, each one detailing Sanitaire's daily appointments. Some of the entries referred to dates that he had kept in the past, while others mentioned future engagements.

Taureau's large square-nailed finger pointed to the day in question. '*Regardez*: "9.30 p.m. James Crack." What do you think that means?'

'I have no idea,' said James Crack. He was, for the first time in his life, truly perplexed. 'It is a code or something, but for what? Oh. Wait a minute; he was supposed to come to my lecture this evening. We were going to have a drink afterward. Maybe that was it?'

'Monsieur Crack. I have seen many deaths in my time as a police officer. I believe when a man is dying he wants only one thing: revenge!'

'But if Sanitaire wanted to tell you who killed him he would have written down someone's name.'

'*Exactement!*' A smug smile spread across the Belgian detective's grey-chopped face. Crack's heart beat a little faster. He felt genuinely uneasy.

CHAPTER SEVEN

Taureau took the book he had been carrying under his arm and passed it to Crack. The tome was dense, perfectly bound and it lay open on page twenty-seven. Page twenty-seven! It was the sacred number of the Mayan Indians. *Surely significant*. There was a pen-and-ink sketch of a castle on the facing page, or page twenty-six.

'It looks like a travel guide,' Crack started. 'Written in, I would have to say, modern English, by which I mean American, in the late-twentieth, early-twenty-first century. Mass produced, quite cheap. I would have to look at the cover to tell you more.'

Taureau was impressed and looked at Crack with a renewed respect. 'You are as good as they say you are, Professor. As you say, it is a guidebook. To Syria, dated 2000. Does the picture on page twenty-six mean anything to you?'

Crack turned the book in his hands. He instantly

recognised the castle by the words underneath: 'Crack de Chevalier'. It was a crusader castle built in the twelfth century. Crack saw that the word 'Crack' had been ringed in pencil. Again, unease welled up within him.

'It is possible that Sanitaire ringed your name to tell us something, *non*?'

'But what?'

'We shall see, perhaps. In the meantime, he has jotted some numbers below the picture. Will you read them out and tell me if they mean anything to you?'

Crack read: 'Zero five five two one four nine five one nine.'

'And zey mean nothing to you?' spat an incredulous Taureau.

'Again, a code. But this is not really my department. You need a cryptologist.'

'Ah, of course! And where do you suppose I will find a cryptologist at this time of night?'

Just then they heard a pair of high heels on marble, their owner walking quickly towards them.

'Professor Crack?' a soft, but surprisingly authoritative female voice asked, carrying the distance between the two without any evident strain. Crack turned and felt his knees wobble. Coming towards him through the paper snow drift was one of the most beautiful women he had ever laid eyes on, her stride languid yet purposeful.

'What is she doing here?' barked Taureau, but the woman ignored him, her grey-green eyes fixed on James Crack. She stretched out a hand.

'I am Agent Raquin, of the Bureau Bibliotechnical En Tout Cas de Bruxelles,' she said coyly. 'The BETCB.'

Crack could hardly think straight. Had he ever seen a more beautiful woman? He took her soft but firm palm and realised he had made a mistake. Her eyes were not grey-green but a deep, almost muddy green, although they were bright and sharp, if slightly crossed. She had a mass of auburn hair that fell casually around her shoulders, a foil to the slight asymmetricallity of her heart-shaped face. Her nose was a perfect *retroussé* button, though, and her lips full and generous. She was wearing a knee-length dark coat, which did nothing to hide her long, fluid curves and the possibility of yet more clothes beneath. She smelled faintly of Johnson's baby powder.

'Emily Raquin, I should say.' Her voice sounded like someone playing Schubert on a Steinway in the room next door. Crack was delighted by her slight lisp.

'Agent Raquin,' snapped Taureau, 'what are you doing here? My orders were clear. No one was to disturb us. Especially not someone from library services.'

Emily ignored the slight. In the 1980s Belgium had introduced a detective inspectorate to the library services after a spate of book thefts across the country, and even internationally, had led to the murder of a librarian. Emily, a girl of less than ten at the time, had, with extraordinary insight, found the murderer by following a bizarre set of literary clues accidentally left at the murder site. The investigation culminated with a public showdown on the floor of the KadeWe, Berlin's famous grocery store. After this success the Bureau's future was guaranteed. Any crimes that might involve any fleeting reference to literature were automatically opened to the Bureau Bibliotechnical en Tout Cas de Bruxelles. Emily was, needless to say, their most gifted investigator, but she was a controversial figure, often accused of witchcraft and 'jiggery pokery'. Her reports, frequently published in paperback, were usually bestsellers.

'When I saw the pictures of the crime scene you uploaded to the Bureau, I knew at once I had to come. You see, Gordon Sanitaire was my *neveu*, my nephew.'

'Agent Raquin! 'Ow can that be? Gordon Sanitaire is old enough to be your *grand-père*.'

'*Mon grand-père, oui*. My father, his brother, was much younger than Gordon's father, who married very young, while my father married very late and then when his first wife and child died in a car crash, he married my mother and I came to them as a late blessing, when he had sixty-five years.'

'I see. Well, that is very interesting, but—'

'Wait a second,' interrupted Crack, unable to believe

his ears. 'That doesn't make sense at all. If your father was—'

'Monsieur Crack!' barked Taureau. 'We do not have time to study the genealogy of Agent Raquin. This is a murder enquiry.'

'But I am just saying that—'

'Silence! Not another word. Agent Raquin, since you are here, and you have had a chance to study it, what do you make of the scene?'

'Oh, I have worked it all out, Capitaine, but before I tell you, I must whisper at length into Monsieur Crack's ear. It is very important that I do this.'

Emily's eyes flashed a message at Crack. He obeyed her unspoken command and turned his ear, bending his knees slightly to accommodate her all too feminine height.

'You are in grave danger,' she whispered, her breath warm and sweet in his ear. 'If you do not follow my exact advice something terrible will 'appen. Excuse yourself and go to the bathroom. Go now.'

Taureau stepped in. 'That's enough, Agent Raquin. Can you add anything here?'

'Yes. Gordon Sanitaire has left us a long list of complicated clues that point, one would at first imagine, to the identity of his murderer, but on closer inspection, appear to be the beginning of something that I predict, from a bibliotechnical viewpoint, you understand, could last almost six hundred pages.'

'Six hundred pages?' snorted an incredulous Taureau. 'Nothing could be that long without a great deal of repetition and *extrapolation fallacious*, as we say in Belgium, Monsieur Crack.'

This last remark was addressed to the professor, who was looking bewildered again.

'Nevertheless,' continued Emily, 'I envisage a doorstopper. Let us begin with these numbers written in the guidebook. I have the solution here, but first of all I need to know exactly where you found it.'

'It was on the desk, near his agenda.'

'Under his agenda? On top of his agenda? You see? It might be a clue. Syria is a country in the Middle East, as you must know. If Sanitaire placed the book, relationally, to, say, any other guidebooks, then he may have been trying to tell us something about his world view, the ethnicity of the murderer or almost anything else. Of course, it may not be a clue.'

'Hmm. Tell me about the numbers,' commanded Taureau. Emily held out a sheet of paper. Taureau stared at it for a moment and then referred back to the Syrian travel book in which the legendary curator had written his demonic code. Taureau assumed a Vesuvian aspect.

Crack quickly excused himself. 'I'm feeling a little dizzy, Capitaine Taureau, would you mind if I quickly used the lavatory?'

'What? Oh. OK. But quickly. Follow the signs.'

Crack made his way along the Grand Gallery towards the steel door.

Taureau turned back to Emily. 'Now, Agent Raquin, do not play games with me! All you have done is reverse the numbers.'

'Capitaine! I am not playing games. *Le* curator is the one playing games. The numbers, once you reverse them and decipher them using the Atbash code, correspond almost exactly to the Bonifacio numbers.'

'The Bonifacio numbers?' asked a dismayed Taureau, wearily pulling up a chair and preparing himself for a long wait.

'Yes. You see, the Bonifacio numbers are a classical mathematical sequence discovered by the ancient Phoenicians in or around the eleventh century BC. They discovered that sometimes the sun shone all day on the shores of Elyria and sometimes it did not, and that there was a direct correlation between these hours and the way bees behave in winter. This information was lost until Pope Boniface discovered some papyrus scrolls in a cave in a small town in Upper Silesia when he was trying to make a bonfire one autumn afternoon. Now, if you take the numbers and reverse their polarity . . .'

Emily continued for several minutes, and the police officer was soon fast asleep, snoring glutinously, his chin resting in the bunched fat of his neck.

CHAPTER EIGHT

Professor James Crack ran the brass tap in the public bathroom of the Grand Gallery and splashed some water on his face. Its temperature – cold – was startling. He stared at his reflection in the mirror. His eyes, usually stirringly oceanic, looked dulled tonight. He glanced at his Patek Philippe watch. It was nearly three o'clock. He had been up more than two hours already and he couldn't see himself getting to bed anytime soon. More water. He was towelling off with a handful of harsh green paper napkins when Emily Raquin entered the bathroom. Crack spun. Under the striplight he was surprised to see that the impression of strength she gave emanated from such exquisitely delicate features. Her eyes sparkled with urgency.

'Please, Monsieur Crack, give me your jacket.'

'Why? What is all this about?'

'You are under covert surveillance, Monsieur Crack.

Or *surveillance cachée*, as we say. It is one of the TDBCFB's favourite methods of interrogation—'

'Wait a minute! What do you mean, "interrogation"?'

'It is their most fiendish trick. They invite a suspect to a crime scene under false pretences as if they want to interview him as a potential witness and they watch him to see if he gets scared and confesses everything.'

'But that's diabolical!'

'*Oui*, monsieur—'

'Please, call me Jim.'

'OK, Jim.' Emily liked the feel of the word in her mouth. 'OK, Jim. But we must be quick. Please, pass me your jacket.'

Crack removed his plaid sports jacket and handed it to Emily. He watched as she quickly searched the pockets. Apart from his black leather wallet, a heavy gold pen (given to him by the publishers of his book *Klues for Klutzes*, a jokey little number that had sold so well Crack had given the proceeds to a mental health charity), his notepad and some after-dinner mints, they were empty. Her nimble fingers then felt along the seams and found what they were looking for: a tiny black transmitter pinned under the lapel. She held it out in her palm. Crack stared in astonishment. He felt his jaw drop. Honestly, he did.

'You see?' she said. 'They know exactly where you are to within sixty centimetres. It is the only reason Taureau let you go to the bathroom alone.'

'But he can't seriously believe I killed Sanitaire!'

'He is hiding something from you. Look. This is a photograph Taureau uploaded to the BETCB—'

'The bibliotechnical guys?'

'*Oui*, them. Us. But look, there is something you have not seen.'

Emily showed Crack a computer printout of a J-peg. It was of the scenario that Sanitaire had arranged in the library, taken sometime before Crack had seen it. Written on the floor just in front of the dead body, in the same dried blood, were words which had clearly been removed by the time Crack had arrived at the crime scene and had not featured in the photo that Dijon had shown him in his hotel room. They hit Crack like a punch in the face: '*P.S. I love James Crack.*'

For a moment neither of them spoke. Crack pulled on the neck of his cashmere turtleneck, uncharacteristically betraying his nerves and releasing a cloud of woody cologne into the air.

'But why did he write this?' he demanded. 'It's absurd. How could he love me? I never met the man.'

'We will come to that, but first, Jim, I must tell you that Taureau is preparing to arrest you for murder.'

'Me? Why? What have I done and why are you telling me all this?'

'Because it is partially my fault that you are here. You see, I believe Gordon Sanitaire left that message for me.'

'For you?'

'Yes. The code he left is so insultingly simple. I told Taureau that they were the Bonifacio numbers – which they are – but they are also, when mixed up like this, by an amazing chance, the telephone number of my *grand-mère* in Normandy. My nephew – I always called him Neveu – wrote them so that the TDBCFB—'

'The Belgian FBI, right?'

'Right. So that the TDBCFB would immediately alert the BETCB—'

'The bibliotechnical guys?'

'*Oui*, of which I am the only one who would recognise the importance of the code, since I am the only one who knew the number of my *grand-mère* in Normandy! It was a message for me. Also, when I saw the photographs, I knew at once that the scenario Gordon Sanitaire had created was from Anna Karenina. My favourite book as a child.'

'Could he not just have phoned you?'

There was a pause while Emily thought about this. Her eyes became opaque with confusion. She shook her head to clear some nagging thought. 'It is a bit more complicated than that. Anyway,' she went on, seemingly no longer sure of her ground, 'Gordon Sanitaire and I fell out ten years ago and we did not speak to each other—'

'Fax?'

'I do not have a fax machine. Nor, I think, did he.'

'E-mail?'

'Neveu was very old school. Listen, Jim, you do not understand. This message was meant for me and me alone—'

'A personal letter? That might have done the trick.'

'The post in Paris is notoriously slow. He did not have a minute to lose.'

'What was so urgent?'

'That is what I must find out. That is why he left that message about you. Together, you see, we must find out who killed him and why. And if I am not mistaken, we need to do it pretty fast . . .'

CHAPTER NINE

Capitaine Georges Taureau of the Toutes Directions Bureau de la Cage aux Folles, Bruxelles, woke from a dream into a nightmare. The words 'so what?' kept buffeting around in his mind. He found himself alone in a library with a dead body mocked up to look like a snowy train crash. His principal suspect – an American professor of Para-literal Meta-symbologistics – and that beautiful but rather boring cryptologist were gone and he was left with a cricked neck and a dry mouth. He struggled to his feet and hurried to the command post.

Dijon, his deputy, was smoking a cigarette, drinking Stella Artois from a bottle and lazily monitoring a laptop computer.

'He is still in the toilet, Capitaine,' he said. 'He must be pretty blocked up, *hein*? I get the same way when I have rich food or I travel anywhere.'

'There is no chance he would have found the transmitter?'

'No. It is still moving slightly. It is strange. Whenever I take a crap I take my jacket off, don't you?'

Taureau sighed nasally.

'But look,' Dijon went on, pointing at the screen. 'It is as if he were straining. He will get piles like that, *non*? Relax, Capitaine. If he had found the GPS tracking device, accurate to within sixty centimetres anywhere on the planet, he would have thrown it in the bin and it would have stopped moving.'

'Hmph. What about Agent Raquin? Did you see her pass?'

'The cryptologist? *Non*. At least, if she did, she did not stop to say hello.'

An old-fashioned telephone rang. Dijon snatched it up. He listened a minute, his face paling.

'Right. I will tell him.'

He banged the phone down and stubbed out his cigarette.

'That was the director of the BETCB—'

'The bibliographical Bureau?'

'*Oui*. He says there is something wrong. It is Emily Raquin, sir. She has gone off the rails. She's a lone agent now, working for herself.'

For herself or for someone else? Taureau intended to find out. But first some food and *quelque chose* to drink.

CHAPTER TEN

Stoat limped across Rue van Maerlant at an angle, the hood of his duffel coat, made from a dense fabric produced in a village not too far from Brussels, obscuring his face from the intrusive closed-circuit cameras that protruded from every ledge. This part of the city, the Parlement district, was a cement and glass jungle, planned and built efficiently enough with workaday security in mind, but it was without charm or the power to please future eyes.

The *Mûre-de-Paume*, the legendary keystone, lay behind the doors of the Central Library of the European Commission. Stoat's mission was to retrieve it. He could not believe they were so close. Brown Owl – who had proved himself to be a man worth obeying and had shown that he had access to VERY SECRET information – had given him precise instructions.

Outside the library were two teenage hookers, their

nubile forms sending a tremble through Stoat that he
calmed by pulling on his suspenders, so that the rough
serge bit into his perineum. All thoughts of lust were
replaced by the sensation of pain. Stoat had given up car-
nality – even with female librarians and bookstore staff –
since becoming a member of the URG. To the outside
world it seemed a great sacrifice, perhaps, but compared
to what Stoat had gained, it was as nothing.

He rang the bell and a receptionist in wingtip spectacles peered through the door at him. Late-night visits
were nothing new – researchers and lobbyists and so
forth – but she did not recognise this man with the red
eyes and white fur. He looked outlandish, like an enormous stoat. Through the intercom she asked to see some
identification. Stoat held up a card. He had taken it from
the limp body of one of this evening's four victims. The
woman peered hard at it, glancing from the picture of
the Asian woman on the card to his fur-lined face in
some confusion. After a few seconds Stoat heard the
door buzz to let him in. He pushed it open, his left hand
descending into the duffel coat's voluminous pocket, his
fingers seeking the cold, comforting weight of the SIG
Sauer.

'Only to serve . . . Only to serve . . .'

CHAPTER ELEVEN

There had been a time when Gordon Sanitaire had meant everything to Emily, but that had ended one October afternoon about ten years ago when she had returned from school one day and found him engaged in an activity that neither she, nor anyone else for that matter, was supposed to see. Their relationship had ended as if it had never been, a mere candle flame extinguished by the sugar-coated breath of a five-year-old child blowing on her birthday cake, and it had left them both in the dark. Rather than endure his blundering explanations, Emily had disappeared for a while, staying with friends, always on the run, never replying to his messages. Eventually she had sent a lawyer to tell him that he was to contact her no more. He had complied with her wishes and she had neither seen nor heard from him again. Until yesterday afternoon, that was, when she had found a message on her answerphone, the voice almost impossibly old, like the rustling of really very ancient parchment.

'Emily?' the voice croaked. 'I 've complied with your wishes for ten years now, but something terrible 'as 'appened and I believe we are both in grave danger. I must tell you something about our family. I will be at the Grand Bibliothèque. Will you contact me there? It is urgent.'

Her family? Whatever could he mean? Except for Sanitaire, her nephew, Emily's entire family – grandmother, grandfather, mother, father, four aunts, five uncles and twin brother – had been killed when she was just three years old, only two years younger than the child used in the candle-blowing metaphor above. They had been on their way to Marienbad, in then Czechoslovakia, when the coach in which they were travelling had been sideswiped by a mysterious lorry on a mountain road. The single witness who remained alive – a ten-year-old boy in callipers – claimed it had been a high-sided lorry with a sealed compartment on the back. This had perplexed the Czech police to such a degree that they had the boy draw the vehicle. The resulting drawing, faxed to Interpol and the International Association of Automobile Manufacturers, was identified as being a Bedford van, of the sort that was used by the British Library services in rural areas throughout the 1950s and 1960s. It seemed unlikely, yet the boy was adamant.

And it had been pure chance that Emily and her nephew had not been with them that day. But now all that Emily had to remember her mother, father and brother was a photograph of them together taken at a restaurant in Segovia, the twins with their arms around each other, mother and father smiling enigmatically into the camera.

Emily had not called Gordon Sanitaire yesterday. She bitterly regretted that now. It was for this reason that she had not shown Crack the final line of bloodstained writing: '*PPS I told you so, Emily.*'

As a bibliotechnicalistic expert, skilled in drawing meaning from almost nothing, Emily had just one question as she stood in the bathroom of the Grand Gallery with Professor James Crack: Why had Neveu brought them together? The only possible reason was that, whether he knew it or not, James – he had asked her to call him Jim – Crack had some information she desperately needed. She had to spend more time with him to find out what the hell this was.

'James, we do not have much time. I can get us out of here, but we will have to move fast.'

'I am sure we can figure all this out with Taureau—'

'Have you ever spent time in a Belgian jail, Professor?'

Crack noticed that Emily no longer called him Jim. He could not hide the fact that this stung. 'Of course not, but—'

'This is Belgium. If Taureau has decided you are guilty then you are guilty.'

Emily's eyes flashed again in deadly earnest and James Crack felt unease well within him once more. *Oh Lord*, he thought. *It seems I am about to break out of the Grand Bibliothèque, Brussels.*

'I need a two-euro piece. Do you 'ave one?'

Crack delved into his pocket and produced a coin. Emily took it and fed it into the condom machine.

'Ah, Emily,' started Crack, uncertainty replacing unease, again. He rubbed the back of his head. 'I don't know if this is the right time or place . . .'

CHAPTER TWELVE

Taureau was standing in the command post, halfway through his second litre of Jupiler lager and third horse-tongue sandwich when the room was rent by the klaxon of an alarm.

'*Jesu!*' he cried. 'Turn zat thing off!'

Dijon jumped to his feet and ran to the control board. He smashed the heel of his hand against a panel of buttons and the alarm was cut.

'*Les toilettes!*' he shouted. 'In the Grand Gallery! A window has been broken!'

'Where is Crack?'

Dijon swivelled and studied the laptop again. 'Still there, but wait! He is moving. My God! He is – I don't believe it! He has broken through a wall into the women's *toilettes*! How? And now, my God! He has jumped! Wait. He is running in circles. Around and around. He must be dizzy! Now he is off again. Quickly.

He is moving quickly towards the Place Quelqueplace!
He must be in a car!'

Taureau unholstered the Heckler & Koch MP5 sub-
machine pistol, capable of firing thirty 9mm rounds in
two seconds, and sprinted down the Grand Gallery to
the bathroom. He kicked the door in, splintering the
hinges, found nothing, double-backed through the paper
snow and rolled under the shutters. He came up on one
knee and, out of habit more than anything else, squeezed
off a burst of three shots. The noise was deafening. There
was a muffled groan from the far end of the corridor as
the bullets smacked into something dull. Taureau did
not wait. He threw himself down a flight of stairs, over
the turn-styles, through the revolving doors and out into
the broad expanse of the Place Quelqueplace.

It was empty.

Where was Crack?

The captain ran into the middle of the square, which
was marked by a drain cover. He stopped.

'Dijon!' he bellowed. 'Dijon! Where is 'e? I cannot
see 'im!'

A head appeared from an upper window. 'Capitaine!
He is . . .' The voice wavered with sudden uncertainty.
'He is right . . . beside you. But . . .'

Taureau spun. Another three shots rang out, destroy-
ing a priceless urn in a niche across the square. A
patrolman was sent sprawling in his efforts to avoid the

flying shards. Another ducked behind a car and took a bead on the captain.

'Don't fire!' screamed Dijon from his window. 'It is Capitaine Taureau. He is just a bit angry. Modern technology has let him down. You know 'ow it can 'appen.'

Taureau holstered his smoking gun and let his arms hang. He was bathed in sweat. He mopped his brow.

It seemed that Crack had flown the coop. But how? And where had he gone?

CHAPTER THIRTEEN

The Central Library of the European Commission, built over the ruins of an ancient temple to the goddess Astrakhan, whose devotees were so fanatical that they reshaped their heads with hot irons and stitched lambswool into the scars, was a repository of texts printed in several arcane languages, often unbound and referring to impenetrable rites and customs of some of the most ancient civilisations the world had ever seen. Its shelves were estimated to contain the sum of human knowledge on a great many matters: passports for fish; straight bananas; sausages that contained more meat than fat; cash payments to agricultural consultants in Provence. People from all over Europe paid others to study there.

Madame Solitaire, a slim young woman wearing wingtip spectacles, a camel twinset and grey skirt, reminded Stoat of librarians everywhere. Only her shoes – pointed and high-heeled – suggested another life, away from books. She was obviously nervous, unsettled, perhaps, by Stoat's appearance. He was used to this, especially in winter, when his fur turned white.

'Can I show you to a particular shelf?' she asked.

'You are too kind, but I find book hunting, like . . .' Stoat paused for a few seconds, 'like masturbation – a solitary pleasure. Why don't you leave me here and I will let myself out when I have found what I am looking for?'

It was not a question.

Madame Solitaire gulped. 'As you wish.'

Stoat watched her as she hurried away into the shadows of the shelving. He grasped his suspenders and gave himself three or four biting tugs. When the tears in his eyes had subsided he made his way through the shelves. Brown Owl had told him what to look for.

Like many of the world's libraries, the Central Library of the European Commission was a functional, charmless room full of shelves holding nothing but books and papers. These shelves were arranged along a north–south axis, but, following a tradition that went back to the ancient Greeks, the shelves were punctuated by gaps, or more properly, aisles. These aisles intersected the shelves at right angles, so that anyone walking down one would, when they looked left, or right, see the shelf end-on where the curator of the Central Library had chosen to place a small symbol, or 'number', so that anyone looking for a particular book could be told on which shelf they were most likely to find it. Then all that person had to do was walk down the aisle and find the number that denoted which shelf they were looking for. Once at the shelf, the books were, as is common in most libraries where the Roman alphabet is used, arranged alphabetically.

But the library also contained some startling differences. A yellow 'guide' line had been printed onto the linoleum tiles of the floor. It led from one side of the room all the way along an aisle, across the floor to the loans desk at the very front, where it looked as if it stopped.

Stoat approached the loans desk. He was very close now. Reverently he removed the rubber date stamp and the ink tray and set them on a shelf behind the desk. He would not harm either. That was iconoclasm.

He thought he heard a noise. He jerked around and levered his gun out. Nothing. He stood for a minute. Still nothing.

'I am alone,' he murmured, carefully removing a road-worker's pickaxe from his right trouser-leg.

CHAPTER FOURTEEN

Emily had inserted the transmitting device in a condom, wrapped it in wads of wet toilet paper and flushed it quickly down one of the lavatory pans. Then she took the chrome bin and cracked it sharply against the window. The safety glass fissured and sagged, but it was enough. The resulting alarm was a deafening blare.

'Quick, follow me,' she mouthed, throwing the bin across the room and dragging Crack out into the Grand Gallery. They turned sharp left and ducked down behind a shelf. Seconds later Taureau came pounding along, gun in hand, and crashed into the very bathroom they had just vacated. A moment later and he burst back out of the door and sprinted back down the length of the Grand Gallery.

When he had gone they breathed again.

'We have not got much time,' Emily said. 'Taureau will soon discover they are following the line of a sewer.'

Crack and Emily got to their feet and approached the body of the revered curator. Someone had turned off the spotlight and his body lay in the eerie glow of the paper snow. It had occurred to Emily that the clues her nephew had left were so arcane, so bizarre, that they might not have been the last thing he had ever written. That instead of being the solution to the problem of who killed him, they were a pointer elsewhere. As if something else were more important than his mere death. But what? *Come on, Emily! Think! What was Neveu trying to tell you?*

Crack picked up the guidebook to Syria and something occurred to him. He span.

'Emily?' he asked. 'Did your nephew ever go to Syria?'

Emily thought for a second. She had been out of touch with her nephew for ten years, ever since that day in October ten years ago when . . .

'Yes!' she remembered suddenly. 'I saw him on a travel programme once. It was an incredible surprise. He was being interviewed about a castle.'

'The Crack de Chevalier? It's a crusader castle, built in the twelfth century near the—'

'That was it,' Emily interrupted, conscious of the passing time. 'Gordon was going through the stage that all men go through when they become interested in the Templars and the Holy Grail and the Sacred Feminine and stuff like that.'

This gave Crack pause for thought. 'OK. OK,' he muttered, putting the book back on the desk. He stared at the body again. What was it about that writing? It looked odd and certainly made no sense. Suddenly it hit him like a blinding flash.

'Emily! Do those sentences look like anagrams to you?'

'Anagrams? Oh!' exclaimed Emily. 'I 'ad not thought of that.'

Instantly Crack had his pen out and was writing down the words in his notepad, rearranging the letters into circles and picking them off one by one.

Blow off the well informed wart h<u>O</u>g smoothie
<u>P</u>liant criminals canoodle
Tidy Histogram

Seconds later he had the solution:

Heigh-h<u>O</u> torment dismal werewolf to blow off
An animalistic droll <u>P</u>once
God I am thirsty

'I think the last one may be right,' mumbled Emily over his shoulder. 'After all that leather he chewed to make his coat, he must have been thirsty, but the other two? They don't make any sense.'

'No, but did you know that the word "anagrams" is itself an anagram of *ars magna*? The great art? They have been in use since—'

'Jim, we do not have much time.'

He thought for a few seconds more. 'OK. Try this for the first line. Follow . . . the . . . beam . . . of . . . of light . . . from . . . the . . . rose . . . window. Follow the beam of light from the rose window?'

'Follow the beam of light from the rose window? That does not make any sense either. I mean – which rose window? Is Rose capped?'

'I can't tell. It is so dark in here.'

'Here. Hold it up to the light.'

It dawned on them both at the same time.

'Follow the beam of light from the Rose Window!' they chorused. Heavenly music and a wonderful pink-hued light filled the library as they both gazed up. Above their heads a beam of light, thrown up by the floodlights outside, shone as true as a lance through the hole that Gordon Sanitaire had made in the library's famous Rose Window. Crack and Emily tracked its path and found that it hit a shelf of books, and one volume in particular: *Captain Corelli's Mandolin*.

'An animalistic droll ponce!'

CHAPTER FIFTEEN

Stoat was about to drive the pickaxe into the loans desk when he stopped. Libraries are places of silence, he thought. I will not willingly disturb the sacred peace of the institution if I can help it. He removed the road-worker's spade from his left trouser-leg and then took off his jacket and trousers, wincing as the coarse fibres detached from his fresh wounds and matted fur. Naked now, except for his heavy brogues and short grey socks, Stoat wrapped the cloth around the head of the pick and started again.

A dull thud and a ripping sound. He made quick work of the loans desk, ripping it asunder with two more powerful blows. Afterwards he stopped to listen.

Where was that librarian? Probably gossiping on the telephone to her boyfriend. Or maybe a girlfriend? Perhaps the girl was . . . Stoat deliberately pressed the tip of the pickaxe into his shin.

'Only to serve . . . Only to serve . . .'

When the crisis was over, he brought the implement down again, this time smashing right through to the floor beneath. He stopped to clear the broken wood, using his feet to sweep aside the detritus that builds up behind any desk: papers, paperclips, rubber bands, dried-up pens, an eraser, some centimes and strange furry dust. Under the desk the yellow line came to an abrupt halt and seemed to disappear into the earth.

Behind him, through a gap in the shelves, Madame Solitaire watched Stoat as he set to work. She had marvelled at his pelt. So, she thought, the Guild has come at last, just as she had been warned they might. She hurried away.

After ten minutes digging and shovelling, Stoat had managed a hole a metre deep and a metre across. Finally the shovel struck something smooth and flat: a compartment. He bent down and chiselled a space around it. His heart was beating fast now. He lifted the lid. He did not know what to expect, but put his hand down and felt something smooth and rubbery. He pressed down to find an edge to grip and there came strange noise, not unlike that of an adult man passing wind. Stoat peered down. Inside the compartment was a dull purple-and-black checked object – a flat circle of rubber, approximately seven inches in diameter, with an outlet at one side. On the face of the object were two words. Stoat lifted it out and read aloud: 'Whoopee Cushion.'

Back at her desk in the lobby Madame Solitaire thought she heard a bellow of rage rent the air. She hung desperately to her phone. It was the fourth call she had made that night.

'Oh, hello,' she said, speaking quickly into the receiver. 'This is a message for *Ze* Grand Master. *Ze* others are all dead and zere is a great big rodent here who has—'

From across the lobby, the SIG pistol spat another of its deadly bullets. It caught the librarian in the head and threw her forward over the desk. She was dead instantly, but not before she had time to break the connection.

Stoat had been tricked. Those whom he had shot the day before had lied to him. He had killed everybody who knew the secret and he had killed a librarian in her own library, surely a grave faux pas? Worse in his eyes was the fact that he had failed Brown Owl.

He took a few moments to remember how they met, in the bookstore on London's Charing Cross Road.

'Stoat,' Brown Owl had said, 'never forget that Wilkie Collins, the man who invented the detective genre and breathed life into the publishing industry with his serials, was also a stoat. Never be ashamed of your stoatiness!'

Stoat pulled on his trousers and cinched the suspenders an extra notch tighter.

'Only to serve . . . Only to serve . . .'

CHAPTER SIXTEEN

Capitaine Taureau sat in the back of the police car and swore into his cell phone. Despite the wailing siren and the flashing lights, the car was stuck fast in a traffic jam on Chaussée d'Etterbeek, in central Brussels. Traffic did not seem to be a problem for James Crack, however, whose movements were being plotted on the laptop by Lieutenant Dijon in the front seat.

'He is moving in a dead straight line, Capitaine! Heading eastwards. He must be on foot, and running like hell. Nothing stops him. He has just run across the Rue Napoleon. Now he is running down the middle of the Boulevard de Waterloo!'

'You're sure he is not in a car?'

'Unless it is a tank, Capitaine. He has just run through an office block.'

'Still heading east?'

'*Oui*.'

Taureau flipped his cell phone shut. The helicopter was on its way, the huge spotlight illuminating the whole of the city in a harsh white glare, and the gendarmes were rushing to cordon off all exits. No one would leave the city tonight, however fast Crack could run.

'Turn here,' he said, tapping the driver on the shoulder and pointing to the right. The driver gunned the car's engine and swerved right with a squeal of tyres. They rocketed along the cobbled Rue van Maerlant, past the Central Library of the European Commission.

'Hey!' the driver cried. 'I just heard a pistol shot!' A new recruit, he stood on the brakes, throwing the capitaine and the lieutenant forward against their seatbelts. Then he slammed the car into reverse and shot back up the street, the powerful engine whining in protest until he braked again in front of the library doors. None of the occupants moved to get out.

'Rosbif!' snapped Taureau. 'What are you doing? Pistol shots happen all the time around here. It is probably a domestic. We can't get involved. Let's go.'

The tyres screeched again and the car burst forward, flinging Taureau and Dijon back into the leather-upholstered seats. Once again, the captain reached for his cell phone and made a call to a London number.

CHAPTER SEVENTEEN

Professor James Crack and Emily Raquin stared at each other in dumb amazement. Crack stretched to take the book. It meant nothing much to him. A story about an Italian soldier and a Greek woman, it had been a tremendous word-of-mouth bestseller. Crack flipped the pages. He did not know what to expect. Another anagram?

A key fell out – plonk – onto the ground.

'My God! A key!' he cried, tossing aside the book and stooping to retrieve the key. It was rough and crudely tooled, with two large teeth at one end but a freaky kind of pentangle thing at the other. A small rectangular label of thin brown card was tied to it with some string. James turned the label over in his hand. On one side someone had written a P intertwined and an O. They were written in biro, and carelessly, as if whoever wrote them had been doodling. Next to the two letters was some flower or other. Maybe a fleur-de-lis? P and O.

'P.O. What does it mean? Could it be another anagram, do you think, Jim?'

James instantly reached for his pen and jotted the letters in his notepad again. Within seconds he had the
answer: P.O. became O.P.

Emily had gone strangely quiet. She took the key from
Crack and turned it over in her hands. 'I 'ave seen zis key
before,' she murmured. 'Once, long ago, before I fell out
with my nephew. I will tell you in the car, but now we
must get out of here.'

Led by Emily, they ran down the back stairs and out of
the back door of the library, as easily as that. They
quickly found Emily's car: a red Lexus with two broad
white stripes running from bonnet to boot and burning
flames painted down each fender to look as if the wheels
were on fire.

Subtle, thought Crack. Real subtle.

Emily slipped through the window – for some reason
both doors were welded shut – and waited for him to do
the same on the passenger side before she gunned the
engine and swung the car out on to Rue Philippe de
Champagne with a long loud peal of 'Dixie Forever' on
the car's horn.

While she drove she told him the story of the key.
For a second Emily could feel the ghost of her dead
nephew sitting in the rear seat – had there been any –
as she thought back to the day that she found the key

hanging from a nail on the back of some door at home. She had been nine years old.

'Neveu,' she had asked Sanitaire, who must have been about fifty at the time and took good care of her. 'What is zat key?'

'Which key? Oh, zat key!' her nephew had stammered. 'It is a secret key to a secret box in which I keep all my secret stuff. When I die, you can have it, if you want, but hey! Let's not talk about it right now, OK?'

Emily had kept her word. Until now. As she told her story she was amazed again at the way time could compress and then expand depending on what you are doing. By the time she had finished her story, Crack was limp with astonishment. But it was Emily who had the questions.

'Do you know what the key is supposed to open?' she asked, shouting over the roar of the engine as they ripped down Slachthuisstraat, hoping that this was why her nephew had brought her together with Crack.

'No. Not a clue.'

Emily could not hide her disappointment.

'But wait a second,' Crack continued. 'Do the letters O.P. remind you of anything? Let me see those anagrams again.'

Emily, who until that morning had been trying to give up smoking – an evil habit, she thought – instantly passed him the J-peg printout of Sanitaire's Anna Karenina scene, which she had by chance tucked into her sweater pocket. Crack stared at the anagrams for a second.

Blow off the well informed wart h<u>O</u>g smoothie
<u>P</u>liant criminals canoodle
Tidy Histogram

'Look, Emily,' he said. 'Do you notice how your nephew has underlined the O and the P? As if they meant something. I am wondering if . . . Wait a minute!'

A lifetime's learning was suddenly crystallised into this single moment. Of course! That was why he had come to Brussels in the first place, to lecture the students of the Vrije Universiteit about the Order of Psion, a secretive sect of writers and librarians reputed to hold information so powerful that no one knew what it was or who they were. The Order of Psion! And until earlier that night there had been no one more knowledgeable on the subject as the revered curator, Gordon Sanitaire. Could he have been the Grand Master of the Order? It was not impossible. Was that why he had been killed?

'The Order of Psion, Emily. Did your nephew ever mention it?'

'Not to me, but I believe he owned one.'

'Gordon Sanitaire actually owned a Psion?'

'Yes, a small 'and 'eld computer. Uh-oh!'

Two police cars from the TDBCFB were parked at

angles across Burgstraat, the patrolmen bristling with heavy weaponry and attitude. Emily braked sharply, throwing Crack against his seatbelt, compulsory in Belgium, even if you are in the back seat, although Crack was not, since this model did not have a back seat. The policemen looked up, like dogs sniffing the air. Who would be about at gone three in the morning and unwilling to approach a police checkpoint? Surely only someone with something to hide. Emily gunned the gas, snatched at the handbrake and tore the car around in a circle of burning rubber. They hurtled back in the direction of the station. Clutching the roll bars with white-knuckled hands, Crack watched through the tiny rear window of the Lexus as the patrol cars surged into life, their sirens wailing and lights flashing. Emily took a hard right, then another, then another, coming back onto Burgstraat only seconds behind the racing police cars. She turned right again, following them only as far as the right turn she had originally made. When they went right she went straight on and lost them.

'Oh, my sacred aunt,' whispered Crack.

'Not bad for a girl, I think?'

CHAPTER EIGHTEEN

Crack and Emily had driven through God knew where until they had found a McDonald's fast food restaurant. Many people despised this company, but the professor knew otherwise.

'I could eat a horse,' he had muttered on their way through the welcoming automatic doors, which had opened instantly to receive them.

'Oh. We will 'ave to find another restaurant, then,' murmured Emily apologetically.

'No. No. It was a figure of speech, Emily. A Joke. I did not mean it literally.'

'Oh. OK. But please, and I know I might regret this, but will you tell me everything you know about the Order of Psion?'

James started even before they had ordered their meal. As usual he was surprised at how little people knew about the Order of Psion.

'The Order of Psion was founded some time in the thirteenth century by a woman named Wolfram von Essenbach, who—'

'Wolfram is a man's name, *non*?' interrupted Emily.

'Yes, that's right, Emily. Many women wrote under assumed names, though. In fact, most of the writers whom you think of as men were, in fact, women.'

'Shakespeare?'

'Her name was Judith.'

'Voltaire?'

'Susan Voltaire.'

'Geoffrey Chaucer?'

'Now Chaucer was a man. He married Giovanna Boccaccia in 1347.'

'Boccaccia? I thought that was a type of bread roll.'

'Very good, Emily, but you are thinking of a bocadillo. It is Spanish. You can have it with cheese or ham. *Queso* or *jamon*. Coincidentally it was named after Maria Bocadillo, who wrote *Dona Quixote* and later married England's Earl of Sandwich, after whom the colour teal is named.'

'But back to the Order of Psion for a minute . . .'

Emily questioned Crack while they collected their food and found some seats. The Order of Psion guarded its secrets well, explained Crack, each member passing the information on to their daughter, or very occasionally their son if they were not blessed with the Sacred

Feminine, and in this way they hoped literature would improve, refining itself with each passing generation. Emily had nearly finished her quarter-pounder before Crack even got to the meat of his impromptu lecture. The fries had been good, the root beer only so-so. It occurred to her to wonder why she had not turned left when she came out onto Burgstraat. She could have dropped the American at the Embassy no trouble.

The Order of Psion was coincidentally the subject of James Crack's latest manuscript, which was currently sitting on his editor's desk in New York. Other than his editor, no one had seen it yet. On his way to Brussels Crack had dropped in at the publishers (where he was revered as a God) and he remembered the interview fondly.

'James,' his editor had said. 'We've had a good run, but you can't publish this. It is too outlandish a theory. You have a reputation to preserve. You are the Catt Butt Professor of Para-literal Meta-symbolist Studies, for God's sake. Do you really believe what you say here?'

'Enough to have done a word search on the world wide web and rung the mother of a friend of mine,' James had replied with an eerily quiet smile. 'Also, look at this.'

He had pulled from his pocket a piece of paper and shown the editor a list of fifty books, all of them academic bestsellers, whose titles hinted directly, or indirectly, at their support of his own theory. There was even a book by Lord Tod Wadley, the famous British historian, rightly considered an expert in the field of para-literalism.

'So it isn't even a new theory?' his editor went on. 'You've just read a couple of these books? And, James, if all these books have already been written, who is going to buy yours? I mean, some of these guys are pretty heavy sausage. Even Lord Tod Wadley is there.'

Crack had smiled again. He had expected nothing less from a publisher. Of course they wanted to keep the secret just that: secret.

'The Order of Psion,' he found himself telling Emily now, 'dates from a more innocent age, an age when writers wrote books that both men and women read. Some of the earlier writers are a bit obscure, but think Charles Dickens. Think Jane Austen. Think Henry James. These writers came from a long tradition that saw certain fundamental human interests were common to both genders, and addressed those issues. Everybody – man, woman and even child – read their books. This was the universe in balance. A man read a book, passed it to his wife; she read it, passed it on to the kid, who read it and then passed it on to his wife, or if it were a girl, her husband. And so forth. Because the books dealt with universalities, they were timeless. As interesting to one generation as they were to the next.'

Emily stifled a yawn and glanced at her wrist-watch.

She had been up for nearly twenty hours and this was the last sort of thing she needed.

'In addition,' Crack went on, 'each of these writers learnt much from the other older members of the Order, refining their books and their ideas, making each better than the last. In this way there was a theory that someone in the future would eventually write such a good book that no one would read anything else – ever.'

'But,' asked Emily, licking the tips of her fingers, 'if what you say is true, wouldn't that put publishers out of business?'

'Exactly, Emily. Imagine a secret that powerful. And so a group of publishers called the English Book Guild – a shadowy organisation operating out of a town called Stevenage in Great Britain, the land of King Arthur and the Knights of the Round Table – was created to combat the advances the Order had made.'

James took a sip of his Coke-style drink. Emily was looking stunned, almost stupefied.

'But within the English Book Guild was an even more extreme group, based at their headquarters in Uxbridge Road, in London, determined not only to eradicate the Order for ever but to drive a wedge between man and woman to further their own demonic ends. This group, with a branch here in Brussels unbelievably enough, realised that they could double their profits if they forced writers to write books only for men, say, or women, or even children. So that men would then only buy books that women would not want to read because they were full of testosterone-fuelled violence in aeroplanes, while women bought books that men would not read because they were about flower arranging and the experience of being a woman, which no man gives a hoot about.'

'So it is a plot?'

'I am glad you asked that question, Emily. Some call it a plot, yes. Others call it a conspiracy. The Guild employed a woman called Virginia Woolf to write a book called *Orlando*, which has more blood on its pages than any other volume in the history of publishing.'

'How can that be?'

'It drove the genders apart. Each was seen in so appalling a light that incalculable numbers of women were tortured to death, while an incredible number of men had their tea instantly poisoned by their previously loving wives.'

'But there must have been women who wrote just for women before? What about Lesbos the poet?'

'Lesbos? David Lesbos was a man.'

'*Mon Dieu!*' cried Emily, gasping and putting her hand to her mouth.

Professor Crack was used to such expressions of surprise. He lectured to students about this sort of thing all over the world. He even took his lectures to prisons as part of his charitable work. The inmates were usually suspicious at first but after sitting a course in his para-literalogisticisms, most hard-core convicts went on to lead full and rewarding lives, even those on death row.

Crack returned to the here and now with a start. Emily was calling him. Her apple pie – caution, contents may be hot – had been eaten and she was halfway through her strawberry milkshake. Value meal indeed, thought Crack. Emily was holding the key they had found in *Captain Corelli's Mandolin*, in the library.

'Jim? Look at the label! Something is happening.'

Crack took the key and studied its label closely. Again he felt his jaw begin to drop. Emily had managed to smudge a tiny dab of her tomato sauce on the blank side of the label, but it was blank no more. The acidity of the condiment must have somehow reacted with something on the paper and some pale marks were beginning to emerge. Could Gordon Sanitaire have used invisible writing?

'Is there any more ketchup?' Crack asked. Emily passed him the remains of the sachet and he applied it to the label. In the harsh light of the restaurant's strip light, spidery characters emerged from the brown, turning from odd disconnected loops into letters and then finally three lines of text. It was an address, here, in Brussels: 'Square Atomium, Boulevard du Centenaire, 1020 Bruxelles.'

CHAPTER NINETEEN

Capitaine Taureau of the Toutes Directions Bureau de la Cage aux Folles, Bruxelles, stood shoulder to shoulder with his lieutenant on top of a high grassy bank, somewhere to the east of the city. A stiff breeze blew in across the flat countryside, chasing the persistent drizzle into his face. From where he stood he could see the lights of the city in the distance, staining the night sky orange. It was four-thirty in the morning, but nothing was peaceful. Behind him were parked approximately fifteen police cars, their lights gently revolving, the officers huddled in groups, smoking cigarettes, passing the time until the next order. Two helicopters hovered overhead, their searchlights illuminating a broad expanse of the circular pools and run-offs. It was the sewage works for the city of Brussels. They had followed the tracking device from the Grand Bibliothèque to here, 15 miles east as the crow flew, and all for nothing.

Lieutenant Dijon was still looking at the laptop. 'He is in that pool there. The one on the left.'

A vile stench hung in the air. Taureau let out a bullish snort of disgust.

'Never mind, Capitaine. It is not the end of the world. We can still find him. The road blocks—'

'Bugger the road blocks, Dijon. I want this bastard and I want him good.'

Just then another officer shouted up from his car. He had been on the radio.

'Capitaine! Capitaine! Interpol. Someone has seen Crack in a McDonald's, in Schaerbeek. And it looks like Agent Raquin is with him.'

'Raquin! That bitch. What is she doing there?'

'Eating a Big Mac, I think, with fries and an apple pie. We are still working on the identity of the soft drink.'

'It does not matter, we will soon find out. Let's go.'

The helicopters peeled away, rotors clattering overhead and beams temporarily extinguished as they headed back to the city. Below Taureau his motorised convoy ground its gears and surged out onto the bypass.

They were going to find James Crack and kick his ass.

CHAPTER TWENTY

The noise of a helicopter flying overhead woke Stoat in his cell on Rue Jeanne. It was barely light. He had chosen to sleep in his serge trousers, a sure sign that even greater mortification than usual was needed. The burning pain in his perineum and his shoulders brought him up short, reminding him instantly of his mental anguish.

I have failed Brown Owl.

In certain extreme circumstances, foot soldiers of the Guild, in search of greater discomfort, were allowed to wear their ties so tight that breathing was a labour. Stoat pulled his own as tight as it would go, feeling his cheeks flushing, his neck bulging and his pulse pounding dangerously in his temples. Breakfast was a quarter of an orange. After five minutes of the corporeal extremis, Stoat loosened the knot in his tie, just seconds before he drifted into unconsciousness. Suicide was not an option for members of the Guild.

He picked up the phone with trembling hands and dialled the number. Again it was answered before the second ring.

'Hello?'

'Brown Owl?'

'Speaking.'

'Brown Owl, I have failed you. All is lost.'

Stoat related the events of the night; how he had found the Whoopee Cushion and been forced to kill the librarian.

'You give up too soon, Stoat. Your faith is not strong enough. It seems that Gordon Sanitaire, the Grand Master, left clues as to the whereabouts of the *Mûre-de-Paume*, the legendary keystone.'

Relief flooded through Stoat's veins. Great indeed was the power of the Guild to know such things. Brown Owl explained that he would call again when he knew more. Stoat was awed again by the man's dedication. But something still puzzled him.

'Brown Owl, something still puzzles me.'

'Speak, my son.'

'Brown Owl, when you use the word "legendary" to describe the legendary keystone, in what sense do you mean it? Do you mean that the keystone exists only in legend? Or do you mean it in the sense that a sport's commentator might use the term, so for example, one might speak of a legendary football player?'

There was a quiet sigh on the other end of the line, a clatter and then the line hummed. Brown Owl had hung up on him. Stoat pulled on his suspenders until he broke sweat.

CHAPTER TWENTY-ONE

Around them the city was beginning to come to life. The streets were being swept, milk was being delivered, men and women were setting up market stalls, and the trams were filling with early commuters. It was a familiar and comforting sight to Emily Raquin as she piloted the Lexus north through the city, following signs to Heysel. Sitting in the leather bucket seat next to her, looking tired now but still focused, James Crack continued to tell her everything he knew about the Order of Psion. She kind of wished he would stop, but what he said was eerily fascinating, if wholly unbelievable.

'Only four men or women at any one time know for certain the Secret of the Order of the Psion – the three *vacherin* and the Grand Master.'

'But what is the secret?' Emily asked.

'No one but those four know, obviously, otherwise it

would not be a secret, but some scholars believe the founders of the Order—'

'Wolfram von Essenbach?'

'Yes, and Thomasina Aquinas—'

'Thomasina?'

'Yes. You remember the Sacred Feminine? I told you about it in McDonald's. Women writers pretending to be men?'

Emily nodded, although in truth she could not think that far back. Her Value Meal was repeating on her.

'Anyhow,' continued Crack, 'some scholars believe the Order was working towards the greatest book that will ever be written. They believe that the secret ingredients of this book – characterisation, plot, setting and so forth – what para-literalists call the Asti Spumante Code – are contained in something called the *Mûre-de-Paume*, the legendary keystone.'

'The *Mûre-de-Paume*?'

'Yes. It is a complicated derivation. Literally it means "the blackberry of the palm". No one but the four knows what it looks like or where it is or even if it really exists.'

Emily pulled the car up at the side of the road and unbuckled her seatbelt. 'This is Square Atomium,' she said simply.

It was a large space, the grass criss-crossed by gravel paths and fringed with trees. They were parked next to a squash court. Crack slid awkwardly out of the car window, banging his head on the sill.

Oh very suave, Jim, he thought.

They stood for a second by the car, wondering what the hell they were supposed to do now. Emily took the key from her sweater pocket. She turned it over and studied the label again.

'One key to rule them all,' she murmured.

'What?'

'Nothing. There is nothing else on the label. Only zis address.'

'We've got to find something that it might open. You go that way, I'll go the other. We can meet on the opposite side of the square, behind that thing over there.'

'OK,' Emily said, confident in his plan.

Ten minutes later, they had got no further. Neither had found any door the key was likely to fit. It was then that Crack looked up and noticed, in the middle of the square, about fifty metres away, a model of an iron atom magnified 150 billion times, so that it looked to be about a hundred and two metres tall, clad in aluminium. An unexpected gleam came into his eye.

'Emily, look!'

The bibliotechnician leapt back in startled astonishment. '*Mon Dieu*! An atom.'

Grabbing her hand, Crack and Emily approached the atom. It was, they soon saw, a building and there seemed to be some sort of visitors' centre at its base. Its doors were made of protective glass punctuated by two long chrome handles but no keyhole. To the left of the doors, shut this early in the morning, was a steel boxed intercom. On the cladding was a small button. Under the button Crack read the word 'Poussez'.

'Poussin was the favourite painter of my nephew,' said Emily.

Crack felt his throat tighten. The Atomium was built on the site of an ancient Celtic temple to Otis, the sun god, rarely seen by Celts – hence the unusual design based roughly on that of an atom, but with a larger footprint – and was said to represent Isis nursing her son Horus, whom she was lucky to have in the first place, given how he was conceived.

Crack pushed the button. There was no response. He tried again. Still no reply. He was just about to give up when an eerily metallic voice came.

'*Oui?*'

Although the professor spoke fourteen foreign languages, he had yet to master French, and quickly made way for Emily, who spoke quickly and persuasively into the intercom. A minute later there was a buzzing sound and Emily pushed the door. It instantly swung open, as if on hinges. They were in.

CHAPTER TWENTY-TWO

They were in a marble-floored atrium. Around them were glass-fronted booths, free-standing ashtrays and posters detailing prices of admission. Crack could hear an insistent noise, as if someone were trying to attract their attention using a knuckle to knock on glass. Then, behind the darkened glass of one of the booths, he noticed a shadowy figure knocking a knuckle on the glass.

'Emily.' Crack pointed. They approached the booth.

An old man, almost impossibly wrinkled and warty, like a cane toad, stared at them like a reptile in a zoo. His eyes were bulbous and walled. He was wearing a shiny midnight-blue suit, with a heavy sprinkling of dandruff on each shoulder; one was lower than the other by a good six inches. He had a string tie, clamped to his throat with a silver eagle. A whorl of dirty grey smoke rose from where a cigarette burned in the ashtray next to him. He looked at Emily as a butcher might study a Jersey calf.

'You really are the aunt of Gordon Sanitaire?' he croaked, his voice fissured by a lifetime's cigarette abuse. 'You look so young.'

He stretched the last word so long as to make it obscene. Crack felt his fists tighten. Let it go, Jim, just let it go. Emily can handle this herself.

'*Oui*, he was my nephew.'

'My name is Boris Cheval. I play squash with him. I always beat him. He is a pussy.'

Crack could stand it no longer. He stepped up to the aperture in the glass, temporarily excluding Emily from the conversation. His voice, which had once been described as liquid chocolate, took on a hard edge. 'I think you mean you *played* squash with Gordon Sanitaire,' he snarled. 'I think you mean you *used* to beat him and that he *was* a pussy. The old man is dead.'

'Dead?' Cheval turned his gaze back to Emily. 'But that is impossible. We have an appointment. I have booked a court. These things are non-refundable.' He pulled a soiled handkerchief from his pocket and mopped his warty brow. 'Why are you here, anyway?' he asked.

'We have a key. With this address on the label. We were hoping you might be able to tell me what it will open.'

Emily held the key up for inspection. Cheval smiled,

then retreated into his booth, out of the direct light. Only his eyes gleamed.

'Hmph. Gordon ever mention me? How I beat him at squash?'

Before Emily could answer Cheval lurched forward suddenly and broke into tears.

'My God! Gordon! Dead! I can't believe it. We were like brothers.'

He sobbed for a minute. Emily looked sceptical.

'I can give you some money if you tell me,' she offered.

Cheval stopped weeping instantly. One eye rolled up to regard Emily grotesquely. ''Ow much?'

'Fifty euros.'

'Fifty euros will not even cover the money I have lost on booking the squash court. Make it sixty and I will show you the keyhole.'

Emily held his winking eye for an awkward second before nodding.

'You will have to buy tickets for a tour of the Atomium though. I cannot let you in otherwise. The full tour is best.'

'How much is that?'

'Thirty euros.'

'Each?'

'Each.'

Emily looked at Crack and shrugged apologetically.

The American reached into his pocket and pulled out his wallet. He produced a sheaf of bills, peeled off three twenties and passed them over. Cheval sniffed them three times before tucking them away in the top pocket of his shirt. He slipped off his seat and vanished into the interior of the building. Crack felt uneasiness well up within him once again. *What the hell was taking the old man so long?*

Just then a door in the wall opened and Cheval – revealed as a squat, twisted man with a club-foot – gestured to them.

'The money?'

'More money?'

'The first sixty was for the tour. This is for the information about the key.'

'Now wait a minute you goddamned European shyster—'

'James!' Emily placed a placating hand on the American's shoulder. It was the first time since they had met that she had touched him and the effect was immediate. Crack thumbed off another three twenties from his fold and handed them over. Again Cheval sniffed, a disgusting sight, and pocketed them.

'Follow me,' he said, turning and leading them into the guts of the building. He was surprisingly quick for someone so ugly. He led them along a series of corridors to a row of sheet steel lockers – the sort one finds in schools and gyms. He showed them to a locker numbered six, the same number as the famous chapter in *As I Lay Dying*, by William Faulkner, a writer neither Emily, Crack, Cheval nor Sanitaire had read, which reads just: 'My mother is a fish.'

'This is – or was, I should say, *hein*? – the locker of Gordon. I rented it to him for his squash kit. He is in arrears, by the way. Three weeks, at twenty euros a week?'

Crack did not even bother to argue. He passed Cheval three more twenties. Again Cheval sniffed them before tucking them away. Crack had other things on his mind. He could feel his heart beating a little faster. Was this truly the keeping place of the legendary *Mûre-de-Paume*? In a museum staff locker? Emily seemed to be affected by the same nerves. She stood there gazing at the scratched steel door.

'Let's try the key,' Crack whispered, his voice hoarse with tension.

The key was suddenly heavy in Emily's hand, but it fit the lock perfectly. She turned it clockwise. Nothing happened. Crack broke a sweat.

'Try the other way,' he said.

She twisted it anti-clockwise and instantly the tumblers fell into place. The door swung open on rusty hinges.

CHAPTER TWENTY-THREE

Capitaine Georges Taureau, like most Belgians, did not like immigrants. His views on the subject were well known and often very forcefully expressed. He stood outside the branch of McDonald's that James Crack and Emily Raquin had vacated less than an hour previously and he stared hard at the boy who had served them their Value Meals.

Taureau was tempted to have this boy – the name-tag read just Iqbal – deported. Iqbal, if that was his real name, had been unable to provide any information beyond what the two had eaten and how much it had cost them. Taureau was about to leave when the boy spoke again.

'Cool car, though.'

Taureau span. When he had squeezed the last details from the cowering economic migrant, he ran back to the car and ordered Dijon to put out an all-points bulletin on the red Lexus. There could be no other car like it in Brussels and, with the police network of snitches and spies so firmly entrenched, they were sure to catch up with Crack and Raquin within minutes.

Taureau rubbed the bridge of his nose and squeezed his eyes shut. He had been up since the morning before and he was now feeling weary. At the beginning of this investigation it had briefly occurred to him that James Crack might be innocent of this crime. At a push the professor might have been able to kill Sanitaire and get back to his hotel room undetected, but he could not have been responsible for the deaths of those other three bookworms. He was, after all, giving one of his lectures to a packed auditorium at the Vrije Universiteit; a water-tight alibi. The professor becoming a fugitive, then, did not really make any sense. It must have been something he had discovered at the library that had set him running. That or something that Emily Raquin had told him. Taureau was just about to order Rosbif to take them back to the Grand Bibliothèque when the car radio on the dedicated police wavelength shrieked into life. Security at the Atomium had just rung Interpol. A man and a woman responding to the circulated description of Crack and Raquin were in the building.

'Let's go!' bellowed Taureau.

There was a percussion of slamming car doors. Sirens started their ominous wail and engines roared to life.

The convoy set itself in motion again and screamed out onto the main road heading north-east, towards Heysel. In the lead car Capitaine Taureau flipped open his cell phone and dialled a number.

This time he would have them. This time he would make no mistake.

Two minutes later, in a book-lined office in London, a man replaced the telephone with a sigh. He stood for a second by a bank of high-end computers and began inputting a long series of seven-digit numbers. There was a whirring sound as a programme booted up, then the man sat and took hold of an ergonomic dual-control joystick. A screen blinked into life before him. The view was of a bedroom. He pressed the joystick forward. The view shifted. A pillow. He pulled the joystick back. The view changed again. An ornately plastered ceiling. The man grunted in satisfaction.

CHAPTER TWENTY-FOUR

In the locker, under a jumble of sports gear and a very old-school Dunlop Pro squash racket, was a grey metal cash box. Crack picked it up. It was surprisingly heavy and – wait, what was that? A glug of some sort of liquid? Was there a bottle in there? He shook the box again. It definitely contained a bottle of some sort. He placed the box gingerly on the bench and bent to study it. It had a small chrome handle on top and exactly eight rounded corners. Instead of a lock with a key there was a combination dial. Four drums each containing the numbers zero to nine.

'My God!' cried Emily over his shoulder. 'The possibilities are endless. Almost. At least nine thousand, nine hundred and ninety-nine, anyway.'

'Where do we begin?'

They had reached 2,815 when the air pressure in the corridor seemed to change. It was the beat of helicopter rotors above the Atomium. A second later they could hear the faintest echo of a chilling sound: police sirens.

'The police!'

Emily looked to Cheval. 'We have to get out of here before the police seal the building.'

Boris Cheval – he really was repulsive, even for a European, thought James – stuck out his fat bottom lip and shrugged nastily. 'Impossible,' he spat. 'There is only one entrance. Unless . . .'

'Unless what?'

'You could leave through the garage.'

Emily turned to the professor. 'But my car! How will we get to her?'

Your car is a 'her'? thought Crack. How's that for the Sacred Feminine?

'You – ah – could buy mine off me,' suggested Cheval, a repellent glimmer in his rolling eye. 'It is in the garage. Fully taxed. Only two thousand euros.'

'Look, we don't have that kind of money—' began Crack.

Emily cut him off. 'You take *cartes de credit*? Credit cards?'

'*Mais bien sûr*. For two hundred euros extra, and another thirty for the petrol. I filled it up this morning.'

'We'll take it,' cried Emily. 'James? Please? Pay the man!'

Crack raised his eyebrows. It is like the Marshall Plan all over again, he thought.

Cheval instantly removed a card reader that James had not noticed hanging from the belt of his trousers and, taking James's offered card, inserted it into the machine.

'Your PIN number?'

Crack knew instantly that he only had one shot at this. Get it wrong now and all sorts of bad things would happen. His fingers hovered over the number pad. He broke sweat. Think, James! What is your PIN number? In a second he had a brain wave. His PIN number was . . . his PIN number! It seemed so easy. He instantly typed four digits into the machine and handed it back to Cheval. The ugly little man pressed a few more buttons, paused for a minute, then nodded. A short scroll of paper – how appropriate, thought James, thinking of the Dead Sea Scrolls, which had been discovered in the 1950s or those others, which had been found a little earlier, the Coptic Scrolls – issued from the top of the machine. He ripped it off and handed it along with the credit card to James Crack.

'The car is yours, although I will have to organise the paperwork later, if you leave me an address? And some money for postage?'

CHAPTER TWENTY-FIVE

When they finally got to the garage, using a small steel-plated elevator, the car that awaited them was a Fiat Multipla. It was painted an odd shade of yellow that Crack was sure had some resonance in pre-Christian art. Cheval showed them over the interior, alerting them to the car's occasional quirks. Meanwhile Emily stood back, holding her nephew's box, twiddling the dials of the combination lock with the ball of her right thumb.

'Quickly, James,' she said. 'We do not have all day!'

James instantly familiarised himself with the car's controls.

Eventually they were ready. James sat at the wheel, Emily in the passenger seat with the cash box on her lap. Cheval was re-counting his money as James put the car in reverse and backed out of the designated parking space. A deft twist of the wheel and they were facing the exit ramp.

'*Bonne chance*!' called Cheval after them. 'Treat her well and she will last for years.'

They waited for the gate to rise and then pulled off, James exercising the gears from first to second to third. At the top of the ramp was a police car. The driver sat at the wheel; his partner was urinating noisily against an iron railing by the side of the road. A long dark stain raced down the ramp towards them. James stalled the Fiat. The policeman in the driver's seat climbed wearily out of the car and set his kepi on his head. Emily quickly covered herself with a grey blanket.

Patrolman Roegier van der Plancke of the TDBCFB had seen it all before. He had been on duty for eight weeks solid. In that time he had not had a single moment of sleep. He was tired. His eyes were small, twisted, gritty and deep-sunk. His moustache was dewed with something. He bent down to look through Crack's window.

'I am looking for an American and a woman,' he said, his voice rough from red wine and his breath toxic with fried garlic. 'They were in the Atomium. Have you seen them?'

There was a tense pause. Crack felt his eyes drawn to where Emily sat in the seat beside him, hidden beneath the blanket. Surely the man can see that the shapely lump was a woman? Crack broke a light sweat before finally answering.

'*Non*.'

Has my accent fooled him? he wondered.

The police officer abruptly stood. His fat fingers strayed to the moist brown leather of his holster, its gleaming muscular pistol unclipped and ready for use. Out of Crack's line of sight a two-way radio threw out some static. The police officer spoke into it.

'Capitaine Taureau?'

There was more static. An answer came. Crack thought he recognised Lieutenant Dijon's voice.

''E is not 'ere! 'E is making a very important phone call.'

'OK. Well. Never mind then.'

The police officer bent down to peer into the car again, the peak of his gold-banded kepi touching the door-frame. He gave Crack a searching look.

'OK. You are clear to go, but keep your nose clean, you understand?'

Crack breathed a sigh of relief, wound up the window and shifted into first gear. He pulled off slowly, as unhurriedly as possible, glancing at the police car in his rear-view mirror. What have I gotten myself into? he thought. Please God, just this once, don't let them chase me with sirens blaring and guns firing.

Under her blanket, Emily muttered. 'Two thousand, nine hundred and twenty-two.'

They drove quietly, apart from Emily's mathematical mantra. When they reached a roundabout, in the absence of any other specific destination in mind, Crack kept them on it – going around and around until he felt dizzy and the Multipla's petrol warning light came on twenty minutes later.

'I keep wondering why your nephew set up such a bizarre death scene,' Crack said as he filled the car with unleaded petrol at a service station.

'You do?' Emily said distractedly.

'Yeah. I mean, there must have been more to it than just telling you that the *Mûre-de-Paume* was in his squash locker. Otherwise he could have left that message on your answerphone. And if the death scene has no over-arching significance then all we are doing is following a list of sequential clues.'

'Hmm. Could be.'

After paying for the petrol Crack climbed back into the car. By which time Emily had reached 9,998. She triumphantly held the box up to him, her eyes shining with the light of discovery.

'James, isn't that just like life,' she said, as she twisted the last dial one click and felt the mechanism disengage.

Crack whistled through his teeth. 'The cunning old rogue,' he muttered. 'Nine thousand, nine hundred and ninety-nine. All the nines.'

Easy. If you knew how.

'James,' Emily said. 'I am nervous. Supposing this is the *Mûre-de-Paume*?'

Crack felt a wave of tension rise within him. The thought had occurred to him, too.

'There is only one way to find out.'

Emily nodded quietly and set the box back on her lap. She slowly lifted the lid. Inside lay a thick leather-bound book and a half-bottle of indifferent-looking Bordeaux.

CHAPTER TWENTY-SIX

The book, when James Crack picked it up, was like nothing he had ever seen before. The binding was of ordinary red leather, but there was no title or information of any sort embossed into its rough surface – no ISBN number even! The paper between the covers was of unusual and differing quality, so that some pages were very thin – like cigarette papers or pages torn from a cheap Bible – while others were thick and almost cellulose, making it impossible to forget that paper was essentially pulped wood. The writing too was unusual. It did not match. Each page was different. The first page was laboriously hand-written, as if by some old monk in a freezing monastery, while the pages towards the end appeared in jumbled type, as if bashed out on an old Smith Corona. In between, some of them were written in pen and ink or quill and ink. The final page was a computer printout. It looked too as if the pages had been added bit by bit, rather than collected together and then bound at a single moment in time. The language was odd as well, as if . . . could it be? It had been written in a language other than American English.

Distant bells were ringing in Crack's memory.

'James?' Emily asked, her voice puzzled. 'Is it the *Mûre-de-Paume*? The legendary keystone?'

'I don't know what it is, Emily,' he answered. 'At least, I can't be certain. I've heard of this sort of thing, but I have never seen one. I did not know they still existed.'

'What is it?'

'It is called a prolix.'

'A prolapse?'

'No. A prolix. It comes from the Latin. It is a fiendishly cunning device originally developed by the Chinese during the Amoy Dynasty – more famous for their use of soft noodles that could be put straight into the wok – which allowed them to preserve firework recipes.'

'But how?'

'It sounds simple. The master firework designer would write down the recipe and then his slave would stick it in a book with any others that his master wished to preserve. After he had done that, the slave was put to death in the most gruesome manner imaginable.'

'I see.'

'But these don't look like firework recipes,' he went on. 'Nor is it written in Chinese, so I think it is safe to assume this is something else, some kind of variation.'

As James turned the prolix over in his hands and flipped through the rough pages, it became increasingly clear to him that this was not the Asti Spumante Code, or at least if it was, it was itself in code. To crack it he would need help. But, again, where to begin? The information could be hidden anywhere within the prolix – in a single sentence, perhaps – but equally it could be spread throughout the book – a word here and a word there. The order of the pages was often the key to the puzzle, but sometimes the key existed independently of the prolix, so that it could be sent separately to the intended recipient and then the prolix dispatched once the key's arrival had been confirmed. Or the other way around. However gifted a para-literalist James Crack might be, unless he knew what he was looking for, there was no way into this particular enigma.

And yet Gordon Sanitaire had left it for Emily.

Why?

What was the old goat trying to tell her? And what was he hiding from her?

With a twist of the ignition Crack started the Multipla again and headed out onto the slip road. Ahead lay the motorway that would take them south towards Luxembourg.

CHAPTER TWENTY-SEVEN

Lord Tod Wadley, British knight of the Order of *Bassineurs*, author of numerous well-respected academic books, acknowledged expert on the subject of para-literalism and friend of James Crack, lived in an estate on the side of Luxembourg's highest mountain. It was expensive and difficult to maintain, but the views were breathtaking. From his bedroom window he could see over his next-door neighbours' roofs, across three fields and a couple of garages that sold cheap cigarettes, to the borders of France on one side, Belgium on the other and, if he went up into the tower and peered through the skylight, Germany on the other. Germany was the home of sweet white wine and the Lorelei, among other things.

That morning Lord Tod Wadley had been lying in bed listening to a radio phone-in programme when his man, Alphonse Briedel, announced that he had visitors. He got up, threw on a brocaded dressing gown and a pair of

antique moccasin-style slippers, and proceeded to the
drawing room where Alphonse had sequestered his
guests. On his way down he had spotted, through a
window, the Multipla parked haphazardly on the gravel
sweep of the drive. When Alphonse opened the double
doors for him, James and Emily sat on a *chaise-longue*
and were appreciatively sipping tea from bone china
cups. Emily almost leapt off the sofa when she laid eyes
on him. Lord Tod Wadley was a dapper little man with a
leathery face and a head that, with the addition of a set of
laces, would have looked like an old-fashioned football.
In addition he was short to the point that his tailor in
London's Whitechapel did not charge him Value Added
Tax on his suits because under European Union law no
tax should be paid on children's clothes. It was the one
good thing that sprang from Brussels. Lord Tod Wadley
chose to pay the tax all the same.

'James Crack! What an honour!' Wadley cried, ignor-
ing Emily's stifled titters.

'No, no, Uncle! The honour is all mine,' affirmed the
American. 'It's good to see you. And this is Emily
Raquin.'

Wadley reached up to her hand and brushed it with his
lips. It was ever so slightly disgusting, like a miniature
truffle pig grubbing among the roots of a beech tree.

'My lady,' he murmured, sending a tingle of revulsion
up everybody's spine.

'Uncle?' queried Emily.

'Never fear, my dear,' cried the lord, straightening up. 'The appellation "uncle" connotes no familial connection or bloodline. My friends – among whom I count young James here – call me "Uncle" and I would be delighted if you would, too. Now, you will excuse me cutting to the chase, as you Americans might term it, James – A-ha! A-ha-ha! A-ha-ha! Ha-ha-ha-ha-ha! My enthusiasm threatens to overwhelm me – what are you doing here in Luxembourg at six-thirty in the morning? Something exciting, I hope?'

James Crack sat back in the welcoming embrace of the sofa. 'You could say that, Uncle. It is rather a long story.'

Meanwhile, Alphonse Briedel had retired to the kitchen and was idly drying a glass with one eye on the television when he saw a picture of the Fiat Multipla, stolen, its owner claimed, from beneath the Atomium in Brussels.

CHAPTER TWENTY-EIGHT

Lieutenant Jacques Dijon of the TDBCFB stood at the top of the exit ramp of the Atomium, his cell phone pressed to his ear. Capitaine Taureau's cell phone was engaged again. He was always on the phone ringing some old teacher of his. It was pathetic. How needy could he be? There was nothing to be done. Next to him stood Patrolman Roegier van der Plancke and the janitor of the Atomium, an ugly, wall-eyed creature called Boris Cheval who claimed that his car had been stolen. A little further away, over by the railings, another police officer was urinating noisily.

'It cost me three thousand euros!' complained Cheval. 'They just took it like that.' He snapped his fingers clumsily.

Dijon turned to Van der Plancke.

'And you didn't see anything?'

His colleague shrugged. 'I saw a man in a car that

matched the description, but I was looking for two of them, not one. And the man didn't have an American accent.'

'And him? Did he see anything?' Dijon nodded towards Van der Plancke's partner.

'Mannequin was checking the undergrowth.'

'Hmph. Well, we have put a bulletin out on the car. Anything unusual about it?'

'The man had a large parcel in the front seat and the car smelled strongly of petrol.'

'Of petrol?'

'That's right,' chimed in Cheval. 'I think there was a leak in the fuel line. I was going to get it repaired today. It costs a fortune at the garage.'

Dijon studied the ground where they stood. There was Patrolman Mannequin's urine, which still flowed, but there was also another dark line on the ramp. Dijon bent to sniff it. Petrol. He fumbled in his pocket for his cigarette lighter and clicked it over the liquid. There was the most delicate whoofing sound and a triangle of blue flame appeared. It separated, going in opposite directions, spreading quickly both backwards down the exit ramp of the Atomium and forwards along the slip road that only hours earlier James Crack and Emily Raquin had taken in their tell-tale car. A trail.

'Let's go!' cried Dijon, leaping into his patrol car and swerving across the forecourt in pursuit of the dancing blue flame.

CHAPTER TWENTY-NINE

'Tell me, my dear, what has James told you about the Order of Psion?'

They were sitting in Lord Tod Wadley's study – the most extraordinary room Emily had ever seen. Although there were four walls, the tile floor was boundless. There were three mock-baronial circular staircases that led to three book-filled mezzanine floors. In one corner was a plunge bath, in another a three-quarter-size mock-up of a Las Vegas casino, complete with a diminutive croupier in an exquisite little uniform, constantly throwing crap dice.

Emily recounted all that she could remember of James's lecture. How the Order had been set up by writers and their daughters to pass on writers' tips and polish their novel-writing techniques to such a pitch that one day one of their number would write a book so brilliant that it would sell millions and render all other books pointless. The secrets of the Order were kept in the *Mûre-de-Paume*, the legendary keystone.

'My dear! And that is all he told you?'

'It seemed enough,' said Emily quietly.

'James,' cried Lord Wadley with a grin, 'did you tell this delightful creature about the English Book Guild?'

'How they have tried to destroy the Order and its secret?' answered James.

'Yes.'

'And about how the Order had to go into hiding, leaving the secret of the whereabouts of the *Mûre-de-Paume* to only four people at any one time – a Grand Master and three *vacherins*?'

'And the other secret? That the direct bloodline, stretching back beyond the marriage between Homer – who was really a woman – and Aesop, exists to this day somewhere in Europe?'

'I may have missed that bit, but all the other stuff, yes, I told her,' replied James, his voice like molten honey.

'Did you bring up the plot to demonise women by making them read about dreary domestic concerns? The chick-lit plot?'

'I did.'

'And the plot to torment men with impossibly thick blockbusters with embossed gold type on the front?'

'I didn't go into specifics, but I may have mentioned it in passing.'

'Well, that seems pretty clear,' Lord Wadley said, standing suddenly and pulling a side table between the divan and the *chaise-longue*. 'So. Dominoes?'

'The thing is, Uncle, we may have found the *Mûre-de-Paume*.'

Wadley span, and stared hard at James and Emily.

'James, that is quite impossible. I have been looking for it ever since moving to Luxembourg fifteen months ago. Look at my shelves – full of books, including all the classics. The clues are in there. I have finished the entire Western Canon, everyone who has ever been shortlisted for the Booker Prize – including that woman who wrote that book about bones in New Zealand – all the Prix Goncourt winners, and all the greats from China, India and the Middle East. The one thing on which they all agree is that the *Mûre-de-Paume*, the legendary keystone, is hidden here in ancient Luxembourg. Now you arrive at the crack – ha! – of dawn from out of the blue and tell me I am wrong?'

At that moment Alphonse opened the door and coughed discreetly. 'Lord Wadley, would you join me in my kitchen for a moment?'

While Lord Wadley was with his man, Emily studied the books on the shelves. There were certainly enough of them. Crack joined her at the bookcase.

'There is something that puzzles me about my nephew and the members of the Order of Psion,' she told him. 'If the Order was a collection of writers, what did my nephew write? Why was he a member?'

'Ah,' Crack said. 'I knew you would get around to that eventually. There really is no better way to put this, Emily, but the thing is, your nephew was really your niece.'

'*My niece?*'

'Yes. And her pen name was Carol Shields.'

It was all too much for Emily. She felt dizzy. The floor pitched and yawed, and she felt herself fainting into the outstretched arms of the professor.

CHAPTER THIRTY

From beyond the French windows, Stoat watched with a twinge of fury as James Crack caught Emily Raquin's long lithe body in his strong arms and, with little apparent effort, carried her to the divan. He watched as the American laid her out and stroked her hair with tender fingers.

I know what I would do with an unconscious girl on a sofa, he thought with a sibilant giggle, pulling tight on his suspenders. In his book bag he could feel the comforting heft of the SIG Sauer, safety on, full of bullets. He also had an apple in case he got hungry.

Stoat had been standing at the window unobserved for half an hour now, ever since he had hidden the stolen Opel at the end of the drive, climbed the razor-wire fence, stolen through the bushes, still wet with morning dew, and found the right window. Brown Owl had called to tell him where Crack and the girl had taken the keystone. He could feel he was very close now. He had not been able to make out much that had been said in the room, but the words '*Mûre-de-Paume*' had drifted through the double-glazing on more than one occasion.

I should shoot them all now, he thought, but Brown Owl had said there would be no more killing. He was to tie them up and take the *Mûre-de-Paume* back to the Guild's house in Brussels and there await further instructions.

With Crack bending over the unconscious girl, Stoat pushed through the unlocked glass doors and, using the thick pile of the carpet to mask his footsteps, he approached Crack from behind.

He hit the professor a stunning blow with his right fist, just behind the ear, knocking him out cold. The para-literalist's body slumped across Emily's, pinning her to the divan. Both of them were now unconscious. Stoat quickly began to tie Crack up, using some duct tape he also had brought in his book bag. He pulled out a strip of the tape, nipped it with his sharp incisors and proceeded to wrap it around Crack's limp hands, but, although he wasn't a clumsy man, Stoat's fingers were not adapted to operations of this delicacy. He applied the tape, but couldn't get it tight. He knew it would not be enough to hold a tall man in the prime of his life, so Stoat unravelled another long spool of tape and looped it around the dozing Crack. He pulled on it, but something gave.

James's lifeless hands slipped out of the noose and very soon Stoat had his own left hand stuck fast to his own right ankle. He panicked. And tried to pull the tape away, but his other hand became stuck behind his neck. Standing on only one leg with one arm stuck fast to his ankle, the other behind his head, he was in an awkward position. With a final thrash of his limbs he managed to gag himself with two loops of tape. He stood for a second, powerless, helpless. Then he felt himself toppling over, the floor rising to meet him very quickly now, and there was nothing he could do about it.

Oh Brown Owl! I have failed you again!

He fell with a sickening thud out of sight behind the *chaise-longue*. At the moment of impact, Lord Tod Wadley came back into the room, the door banging behind him.

CHAPTER THIRTY-ONE

'James!' cried the Briton. 'How could you? You have abused my hospitality under false pretences! You come here pretending to be interested in talking about the Order of Psion, while you are in fact on the run for murder. It's a bit off, what?'

The professor was rubbing his head in confusion while Emily – crushed somewhat by James's dead if well-toned weight – was gasping for water like a fish in oxygen. What the hell had happened to them? Crack wondered. All he knew was that he had a headache.

'Uncle,' he mumbled. 'I can explain—'

'It is a bit late for that, old boy. Kindly see yourselves off the premises.'

Crack could not resist one of his famous irresistible smirks. 'We came to tell you that you were right about the *Mûre-de-Paume*.'

He had his lordship's attention now. Wadley's eyes were gleaming.

'What? It's in Luxembourg?'

'And closer than you think.'

'Where?'

James Crack pulled the cash box from under the divan with a quiet smile. 'Right here,' he said.

The gleam in Lord Wadley's eye dimmed. 'James,' he said, 'that is just a cheap cash box, the sort they sell in any stationery store. I hardly think the great writers of the past would want to see the secrets of their work kept in such a proletarian vessel.'

'Nevertheless, Lord Wadley,' murmured Emily, waking now, 'there is something inside with which we need your 'elp.'

'A prolix,' said James, pulling out the inelegant-looking book.

Lord Wadley stared at it in shock and then leaned forward to take it carefully in his very small hands. He began leafing through it.

'This first page is written in what looks like Sanskrit. This next is written in Greek. Pre-demotic, I might add. There is rather a lot of that. Hellenistic, by the looks of things. Not very fluent with that, but look – this word keeps cropping up.' Wadley pointed to a word on one of the earlier pages of the prolix: αγψρτία.

Crack shrugged. 'It's all Greek to me,' he joked.

Lord Wadley snorted with laughter and tears of merriment filled Emily's eyes.

'You certainly can crack 'em, James!'

Laughter filled the air for a few minutes before Lord Wadley screwed his monocle back in place and bent over the prolix again.

'I believe it is the ancient word for Tuesday. Strange. Look here it is again. Tuesday. What does that mean, I wonder?'

It suddenly became crystal clear to James.

'I believe this must be a diary of some sort, Uncle. Tuesday is a day of special significance for writers, Emily.'

'Oh. Why?'

'Traditionally there was no fish on the Monday, because the boats had not been out on the Sunday, so the fishermen went out on Monday which meant you could get fresh fish again on Tuesday. Fish is good for the brain. The scribes used to say that it helped concentration and when the first playwrights started putting pen to paper they adapted many of the practices of the scribes. Lucky Tuesday was just one of many.'

'Yes,' continued Lord Wadley. 'Desks and pens and pieces of paper were others.'

The lord flicked a few pages of the prolix until he found the word again. He began a faltering translation.

'"Tuesday" – and there is a number, here . . . four, I think, yes. That's it. "Tuesday, 4 September. Spent the day with a carpenter looking at designs for wooden horse. Still can't see how they did it. Must remember to buy new sandals." How strange.'

'Does it mean anything to you, Uncle?' James asked.

'Not a thing. I'll try another page.'

Lord Wadley flicked through.

'Hmph. This is Latin. Never liked Latin. Let me see, though. Tuesday again. The word "*purgamentum*", Emily, was sacred to Roman writers.'

'But it is not the *Asti Spumante* Code, do you think?' asked Emily.

'I don't think so, my dear. But it might be something to do with it, a companion piece if you like. It gives an inkling into the creative process, of course, but is that all there is to it?'

'It must tell us something beyond cures for writers' block,' declared Crack. 'It can't be a dead end. Otherwise Gordon Sanitaire would not have led us to it.'

But a gleam had again entered the eye of the old peer of the realm. 'I wonder if you aren't right. Listen to this: "Tuesday, 8 Augustus. Idea for a story: man escapes from Troy only to be shipwrecked on N. African coast" – open brackets – "say" – close brackets – "where he falls in love with maybe a Phoenician woman, queen" – question mark – "who is building city."'

'It sounds like the *Aeneid*,' whispered Emily softly.

'Shhh, Emily,' cautioned Crack. 'Uncle is trying to think.'

'This is not just about the creative process, James; it is a clue to the keystone's whereabouts after all. Look: "N. African coast" is obviously a code for Luxembourg.'

Crack thought back to the manuscript he had left on his editor's desk in New York. Was it too late to make any changes? 'Can you make out any more?'

'Hmm. This looks like Anglo-Saxon. Again, a diary entry. This writer is moaning about having run out of inspiration, and going on about someone called Grendel being dead. What does it say? "Everybody says there should be another one but I just can't be bothered. Mother coming to stay tomorrow."'

Emily opened her mouth to say something but at that moment, from his position behind the *chaise-longue*, Stoat let out a muffled cry.

'Good Lord,' cried Lord Wadley. 'Was that you, James? I know you are a man of many parts, but ventriloquism?'

Crack peered over the back of the *chaise-longue*.

'Is this yours?' he asked, picking up an arm of the recumbent ex-bookseller.

Tod Wadley scrambled up onto the sofa and peered over the edge. 'Good Lord, no! What is it, do you think?'

He prodded Stoat with a tiny bony finger. Just then Alphonse came in.

'Sir? I think you should have a look out of the window.'

'The window? Very well, Alphonse, but if this is one of your silly jokes . . . In the meantime, can you pick up that fellow from behind the *chaise-longue*? He seems to be in some difficulty.'

James Crack was already at the window next to Emily. He felt the familiar unease welling up within him. Across the estate's sweeping lawns, beyond the gate, was a sea of blue flashing police lights. The TDBCFB. How in God's name had they tracked them here?

'We had better get going,' he said urgently.

'But, James. Wait. What is that?'

Emily was pointing to a small blue light that Crack had, until then, not noticed against the police lights. It was petite, perfectly triangular in contour and it was dancing up the gravel drive towards them as they watched.

'Is it a flame?'

So that was how the TDBCFB had found them, Crack guessed, remembering the plummeting petrol gauge, but his thoughts were interrupted as the flame reached the Fiat Multipla. It seemed to pause under the vehicle, expand for a second and then there came a series of deafening explosions as fire tore the car limb from limb, tossing it into the air and throwing it down in a cascade of falling automotive parts on Lord Tod Wadley's garden.

'My roses!' he cried.

'*Zut*,' said Emily simply.

CHAPTER THIRTY-TWO

On the other side of the estate's gate, Lieutenant Jacques Dijon of the TDBCFB took the cell phone from his ear and watched in disbelief as the Multipla dismembered itself before his very eyes. His men involuntarily flinched. A pall of smoke drifted across the quiet Luxembourgoise countryside.

'Right! Pull that gate down!' Dijon ordered and returned to his phone. Why was Taureau always busy? He had been trying his line constantly since he had sped down the autoroute in pursuit of the blue flame, which had led them inexorably to Crack and Agent Raquin.

Behind Dijon a small conference of officers convened to discuss how to flatten the gate. Eventually they decided it might be best to ram it with a car and, after five minutes of playing 'Scissors, Paper, Stone' to find the loser, patrolman Rosbif was chosen to sacrifice his car.

'*Pas juste*' were his last words as the police-issue

Peugeot 205 crashed through the gate at exactly 39 kmph, writing itself off in the process. The other patrol cars then poured through and, with their sirens wailing, swept up the gravel drive to where all that remained of the Multipla was a burnt-out skeleton of blackened metal and charred rubber.

'Surround the 'ouse!' cried Dijon. 'I want these bastards alive.' He redialled his chief.

Taureau answered immediately this time. '*Oui?*'

'Capitaine! We 'ave them! They are like rats in a trap.'

'*Bravo*, Dijon! But do not harm a hair of their heads, you understand? There must be no one keeeeled!'

Just then there was a barrage of gunfire from behind the hangar-sized garage to the left of the main residence. Dijon snapped the phone shut, unholstered his own Heckler & Koch USP Elite handgun (which he had bought from an online auction site for just $1,200 – a substantial saving, although he was disturbed to see that customers who had bought the USP Elite handgun had also bought a set of three black Samurai swords) and sprinted around to the back of the garage. His men were crouched in line as if at a firing range, vainly shooting towards the rapidly disappearing high-strength polypropylene cluster lights of a top-of-the-range Range Rover with four-wheel-drive, standard transmission and a steering wheel on the right.

CHAPTER THIRTY-THREE

Alphonse Briedel was not so good a driver as Emily, but Lord Tod Wadley, reasonable in so many other things, would not permit himself to be driven by a woman. The peer of the realm sat in the luxuriantly appointed and heated rear seat of the Range Rover, still attired in his dressing gown and cotton poplin pyjamas, flicking through the prolix page by page. Next to him, deep in thought, sat American para-literalist James Crack. He was still trying to understand the revered curator's meaning in leading them to the prolix. Why had he given it to Emily? What was he trying to say?

'Where are we going, Lord Wadley?' asked Emily from the front seat.

'Britain, Emily,' said the Briton. 'I'm done with Luxembourg. She let me down by not being the home of the *Mûre-de-Paume*, and anyway I've suddenly recalled the myth that the legendary keystone is hidden in Britain.'

There was a muffled question from the back where Stoat lay bound and gagged.

'Be quiet, you,' snapped Lord Wadley, reaching around and giving one of the ex-bookseller's suspenders a sharp tug. Stoat's eyes brimmed with tears.

'Hey,' said James, 'do that again. I think he really likes it.'

No one was yet sure who or what the Stoat was, but Lord Wadley had thought it wise to bring him along with them, just in case ('You always need a stoat'). Alphonse meanwhile steered the Range Rover (still top of the range) into the sunrise, heading west across the border into France, making for Calais and its connections to the island over the sea, the one criss-crossed with ley lines, and through which ran the Greenwich Meridian, the earth's second most sacred prime meridian.

'I confess myself at a loss with this prolix though, James,' Lord Wadley declared. 'It's just ream after ream of diary entries. I've been leafing through it and it is interesting in parts – someone here writing in Middle English that they have a great idea for a collection of short inter-linked stories about some travellers but can't think of a way to give them a common thread – but what does it all mean?'

'Can I see it?' asked Emily softly.

Lord Tod Wadley passed the book to her. Emily's tender hands caressed the leather cover and she felt, for a moment, the ghost of her nephew seated beside her on the Range Rover's body-contoured leather seats. *What is it, Neveu? What are you trying to tell me?* No answer. She opened the book at random.

In spidery writing she found an entry that startled her: 'Thursday, 14 October, Year of Our Lord 1858. Estimable idea for an entertainment on the subject of Paris and London but am unable to conjure up title or first paragraph. Fear muse has deserted me.'

'James,' she said, 'could these diaries come from famous writers? This one – it mentions some coalminers in the Alsace, but the author fears it might be deadly dull – sounds like Emile Zola. And there are more.'

'Zola? Did you know, Emily, that Emily Zola was one of the *vacherins* in the Order of Psion?'

'What about Charles Dickens?'

'Charlotte Dickens? Yes. Together with her lover, Alexandra Dumas, they brought up little Janice Joyce. No one knew who the father was, but some scholars believe it could have been Jane Austen, who was also a Grand Master.'

'Grand Master?' asked Emily. 'Don't you mean Grand Mistress?'

'It is complicated, I know, Emily, but Jane Austen was actually a man. She played soccer for England, too, against Scotland. A useful crosser of the ball, apparently, with what scholars call "quick feet".'

Emily quickly looked down at the book and flipped on a few pages. 'Could this be Jane Austen's writing?' she asked with a gleam in her eye that intrigued Crack. Was she on to something here? Was a pattern beginning to emerge? He took the book and studied the entry Emily showed him. The ink had faded somewhat, but the hand was in fine italics, with purposeful loops: 'Tuesday, 13th March. Raining again. No football practice. Rather bored with MP. Not sure if Fanny is not too obvious a name for such a drip of a heroine.'

'It's possible, Emily. But why? Why would Gordon Sanitaire give us an anthology of diaries by writers?' He handed the book back to Emily.

'Maybe they were all members of the Order of Psion?'

There was silence in the back. It occurred to Emily that the two men had stopped listening to her. In her vanity mirror, she could see that they sat staring out of their windows, sipping on Bloody Marys and crunching on the celery sticks and quails' eggs that Alphonse had passed around earlier. Emily flipped on through the prolix until she came to the last page. With a jolt that even startled Alphonse at the wheel she recognised the computer paper Neveu had always used. On the page were typed two words – 'Under' and 'Cover' – and a sentence that read: 'No marks for coming third.'

CHAPTER THIRTY-FOUR

Lord Tod Wadley, famous royal para-literalist and author of numerous weighty bestselling tomes on the subject, kept a private carriage on Eurotunnel. While those who pay the ordinary price to travel under the Channel have to approach their carriages on everyday tarmac, the surface of Lord Tod Wadley's private lane at Coquelles, Pas de Calais, France, was gently padded to protect the undercarriages of his fleet of off-road sports utility vehicles. His Range Rover, which, on the short journey from Luxembourg to Calais, had been superseded by another even slicker model, purred into the customs post where it was immediately surrounded by agents of Lord Wadley's private customs office.

The men quickly valeted the car inside and out. No questions were asked as to the provenance of the large Stoat bound and gagged in the boot, the SIG Sauer P228, the four hand grenades hidden in the mini-bar, the stack of hardcore bestial porn, the high-grade heroin in the glove compartment or, carefully strapped into each wheel arch, the four illegal immigrants of undetermined origin.

'Welcome aboard, sir. The 07.58 shuttle departure is due to leave on time.'

Alphonse pulled the car up the ramp padded with organic silk and steered carefully to the middle of the carriage where he was stopped by a bowing Japanese woman in a kimono. He turned off the cluster lights, wound down the windows an inch and killed the engine. James Crack could not help notice that the walls of the train were panelled in rare hardwood. It was like the library of a gentleman's club, he thought. The train pulled out almost immediately and seconds later they were in the dark of the tunnel. The car's interior lights fluoresced and they were bathed in a warm glow.

Crack leaned forward to tap Emily on the shoulder. 'The tunnel is exactly 50 kilometres long, Emily,' he began. 'With 39 kilometres of that under the sea – the longest undersea tunnel anywhere on the planet – and these trains are the most powerful we've got. They aren't pretty, but they can generate up to 7,500 horsepower and can move loads of up to 2,400 tonnes as fast as 140 kilometres an hour.'

'Really?' asked Emily inquisitively.

'Yes. About 112 million people travelled through it

between AD 1994 and AD 2000. It is also the market leader in pet travel. Some 50,000 dogs and cats used the tunnel between February 2000 and June 2002 thanks to the Pet Travel Scheme.'

'Oh, yes?'

'Yes, before they had to travel UNDERCOVER.'

Something rocketed through Emily's unconscious mind.

Undercover?

Her fingers urgently stroked the back of the book as she held it. Wait a second. Was there . . .? And then she saw it.

Undercover.

Literally that: just under cover. Under the cover. Or, more properly, under the covers! She closed the prolix and held it up to the lights, letting the soft glow fall on the bottom edge of the binding.

James Crack stared over Emily's shoulder. He too saw that there was a pale strip sandwiched between the two layers of leather, as if they were a cover encasing some card. Could the leather binding of the prolix be a variation of a standard dust jacket, just as one would find on any commercial hardback?

Emily dexterously slipped a finger up under the leather and began to pry it away from the card beneath.

'Careful, Emily, you don't want to rip it!' cried Crack encouragingly from the back seat. Next to him, seeing what Emily was trying to do, Lord Wadley gave a long blast on a copper hunting-horn that he kept in the pocket of his brocade dressing gown.

'Tally-ho!' he cried at the top of his voice. 'The chase is on!'

It gave easily enough; at one point it seemed too easily. Emily's elegant finger separated card from leather, feeling the strands of paper glue stretch and break under the pressure of her digit. After two minutes she was able to separate the two covers. She put the leather cover aside and first concentrated on the prolix, naked now, in the flattering light of the Range Rover. Beneath the leather's protection were thick card flaps.

'A simple exercise book! Just as an author might use for notes,' whispered Crack.

The card was buff coloured and unmarked except for — what? A small patch of plastic. Could it be Sellotape? Emily flipped the book over. There it was: a rectangle of paper approximately five centimetres by three, laminated to the back of the prolix. On the piece of paper were a set of lines of differing widths and heights that could be read from right to left, or left to right, or not at all. It was a code. A barcode.

Underneath were just two words: Uxbridge Road.

James instantly stretched forward to take the prolix in his hands. He examined the barcode with swelling surprise. For a second he was filled with relief at the discovery. So the old fox had wanted them to see this. But the next instant he realised, with a creeping feeling of dread, exactly what the words below the code meant. Uxbridge Road. The home of the armed wing of the English Book Guild. It was a warning. If Gordon Sanitaire had mentioned Uxbridge Road, it could only mean one thing: that the URG had been responsible for his death and was active again, spreading its influence ACROSS THE WORLD.

CHAPTER THIRTY-FIVE

At the other end of the tunnel, Richard Kidney, Chief Sheriff of Kent, acting on a tip-off from a Capitaine Taureau of the Toutes Directions Bureau Bureau de la Cage aux Folles, Bruxelles, had set up a track-block on a quiet cutting in the rural heart of England's most south-easterly county. Parked across the line were two BMW five-series police cars with stick transmissions that belonged to the Kent County Constabulary, while in the bushes around the track, armed men of the Special Response Group (Kent) were setting up sandbags and digging platforms for their eight powerful L1A1 12.7mm heavy machine-guns. These weapons, updated versions of the Browning M2 'Fifty-cal' – recognised as one of the finest heavy machine-guns ever developed – had recently been enhanced with a new 'soft mount' (to limit recoil and improve accuracy) and a quick-change barrel. Capable of delivering 635 rounds a minute, there was no way the train would get through. And this was just the first line of defence.

Kidney was a beefy man of what his father – before he was killed in the Western Desert sometime before the battle of Tel El Kebir – might have described as 'good yeoman stock'. He wore his salt-and-pepper hair short and his horn-rimmed glasses gave him the air of a cattle market auctioneer with stories to tell. He drove a dove-grey Jaguar and was looking forward to a retirement spent on the Tonbridge golf course. This was his last show and he wanted it to be a good one.

He had placed the support artillery carefully, with overlapping enfilading fields of fire so that, if needs be, he could order the destruction of any trace of life on the train should it not stop. Further up the track – as a back-up – he had called in air support. Three MH-60K helicopter gunships hovered a mere foot above an Ashford playing-field, their pilots and gunners ready to respond at a moment's notice. Kidney did not even want to think about the firepower that these machines could bring to bear, but it was still not quite enough. Beyond them, on the other side of Ashford, the track was laid with anti-vehicle mines with extra-sensitive fuses. If the train got through that, Strike Command at Biggin Hill was on standby to scramble a squadron of Tornado jets armed with depleted uranium Tomahawk missiles. His next port of call, should the train still be running, was the Royal Navy. Two type-42 destroyers were standing off the Isle of Sheppey, ready to fire a salvo at the train as it approached London. His final precaution had been to place HMS *Conqueror* in the Thames, its nuclear device, the use of which had been authorised by the PM, primed and aimed at Waterloo Station.

It was true that he was slightly misusing his powers under the Illegal Immigrants Act (2005), but nobody would be able to say that Dicky Kidney went down without a fight.

CHAPTER THIRTY-SIX

Meanwhile, further along the track, some eight hundred feet below sea level, in a private carriage of the 7.58 a.m. Coquelle–Folkestone Eurotunnel shuttle, Alphonse Briedel was sitting in the front seat of the Range Rover listening to some light classical music on the quadra-phonic stereo system. It was set to 107.6 MHz to receive travel updates and information about Eurotunnel services and offers that might be of interest to anyone travelling to or from the Continent when there was an interruption. Alphonse listened carefully to what followed, a bird's foot of a frown gathering at his brow.

'Sir?' he called back to his Lilliputian owner. 'There is going to be an unscheduled stop. Apparently the British police have set up a track-block and are going to search the train for illegal immigrants. Just south of Ashford.'

Lord Tod Wadley smiled slightly. 'Sounds a bit fishy. It couldn't be your friends from the TDBCFB, do you think? Tipped off the Kent police that we are on our way?'

Crack did not know what to think. He was tired now. He had been up all night with Emily, thinking hard, and now all he wanted was to curl up and go to sleep like a dog. Instead here he was sitting in an almost top-of-the-range Range Rover with an English lord and a beautiful Belgian bibliotechnician, a large Stoat and an obsequious manservant. He was on the run from the police and, it seemed, someone else was looking for the *Mûre-de-Paume*, the legendary keystone, perhaps to seize it for themselves and use its powerful content to their own ends. He had to find that keystone. He had to find the Asti Spumante Code, whatever else he did. He picked up the prolix again. He felt he was nearer the goal that the revered curator had left him, but he was all too aware that there was still a long way to go.

'James,' said Emily softly, interrupting his reverie, 'this prolix cannot just be a warning about the Uxbridge Road Group, can it? Or the trail grows cold, *non*?'

'The barcode is the clue,' agreed Crack. 'It is unlikely that a common or garden exercise book like this would have a barcode, so it must be important. But what does it mean? And how do we read a barcode?'

'I have a contact in the business who might be able to help,' interjected the diminutive aristocrat. 'But we need to get to London first.'

CHAPTER THIRTY-SEVEN

Capitaine Taureau and Lieutenant Dijon crossed the English Channel strapped into the back of an Aérospatiale Westland Lynx helicopter, one of the fastest helicopters ever produced. They made landfall just north of Dover and headed inland at an altitude of 1,400 feet, making for the town of Ashford, Kent, a distance of about twenty-five miles. The helicopter came down in a field of corn about half a mile to the south of the town, just above a cutting through which snaked the tracks of the London–Folkestone railway line.

'That is the last time I go in one of those machines, Lieutenant Dijon,' snarled Taureau. 'I would like to strangle whoever invented them.'

They crossed the field, their feet gathering clods of mud as they went, and approached the lip of the cutting. A handful of police vehicles were clustered by a five-bar gate and a light rain had begun to fall.

A British constable pointed them to where Richard Kidney had set up his command post, high above the railway cutting. Above the Sheriff's head loomed the barrel of a powerful piece of field artillery, which was aimed at the exact spot the track disappeared into a tunnel under the M20 motorway. This was where the train would come from. Kidney greeted them cordially and suggested they take up position next to him.

'If you know how to fire a mortar, so much the better,' he muttered, his eyes glued to his binoculars. The sense of expectation and urgency among the camouflaged snipers and machine-gunners as they waited for the train was tangible.

There was a crackle on the radio. The train was coming.

'Show time,' grinned Kidney, getting to his feet. 'Stand by!' he bellowed to the troops around him, raising his right arm in signal. The ground started vibrating. Above the sound of the approaching train all they could hear was the cocking of weaponry. Dijon stared panic-stricken at his boss. Taureau shrugged nervously.

'Sheriff Kidney,' he began hesitantly, 'we are supposed to just stop and search, non?'

'New powers from the Home Secretary, old boy,' intoned the British police officer stonily. 'Intend to use them before I pass on the mantle.'

The train erupted from the tunnel but already it was

slowing down in preparation for the halt. It was an enormous beast, grey and aggressive, with yellow markings, and the waft of heat that poured from its great engines made the air shimmer. The sheer size of it dwarfed the men that stood facing it as if it were an elemental force of nature confronting man's puny physicality.

Kidney kept his arm up.

The train juddered to a halt inches from the BMWs across the line. Nothing happened for a full three seconds. Kidney looked disappointed. There was an audible groan of frustration around the cutting. Taureau and Dijon each let out a long garlicky sigh of relief.

'Right. Let's get them, then, shall we?' said Kidney. He stepped jauntily over the sandbagged wall and began side-slipping down the steep slope to where the driver and the controller – a fat man – were climbing down from the engine. Capitaine Taureau made to join him.

'But Capitaine,' hissed the lieutenant, catching his superior's arm and pointing down to the train below them. 'This is the Eurostar. It is for foot passengers only. I understood that Crack and Agent Raquin were travelling by car? They would have taken the Eurotunnel and got off the train at – 'ow you say? – Folkestone.'

'What?'

Dijon's second attempt at an explanation was cut

CHAPTER THIRTY-EIGHT

Emily Raquin was still thinking about the barcode as they passed some sort of military exercise by the side of the motorway. Heavy tanks were manoeuvring at high speed across the fields towards them and a helicopter rattled overhead. Could they be after us? she wondered briefly. They were heading to London to show the prolix to Lord Tod Wadley's contact in the book trade, and very soon they were crossing Tower Bridge, built by the Romans to commemorate Horatio's gallant exploits against the army of Tarquin. A ship's horn sounded below – a plaintive, mournful sound in the dense fog that habitually shrouded the banks of the River Thames and had given rise to the name of a superior brand of American rainwear. Emily yawned like a cat. She had been awake for more than twenty-four hours now, and was beginning to feel it.

'Left here,' snapped Lord Tod Wadley, as Alphonse steered the Range Rover slowly down Regent Street

towards London's Shaftesbury Avenue. They turned
sharply into the dedicated bus lane of a road the name of
which Emily missed. A couple of hundred yards further
along, Lord Wadley slapped Alphonse's leather headrest
as a signal to stop and they pulled up in front of an old-
fashioned-looking bookstore, with two wooden
bay-fronted façades and a gold-lettered sign adorned
with numerous royal crests. Significant, thought Crack.
It was still very early in the morning and the bookstore
was not due to open for another hour. A man in a long
green apron and a gleaming silk top hat was polishing the
brass push plates on the doors.

'Emily, my dear,' said Lord Tod Wadley with a cunning
glint in his eye. 'I have a plan . . .'

When they were all agreed, Wadley screwed in his
monocle, tightened the dressing-gown cord around his
waist and stepped out of the Range Rover. When the man
polishing the door caught sight of his lordship, he went
pale and bowed from the hips, dropping his yellow duster
and removing his hat with an unconstrained flourish.

Jeez, thought Crack, regarding Tod Wadley's distinc-
tive stature and miniature spherical head, the old boy
must be pretty well known. Lord Wadley allowed his
knuckles to be kissed, patted the man on the head in
benediction, then beckoned them over. The man
straightened and regarded the good-looking youngish
couple with interest.

'Emily, James,' began Lord Wadley, 'this is Donnie Dogs, manager of this fine establishment. I was just saying that we are on our way to see the Queen and naturally wanted to buy her a little something as a hello-thank-you-for-having-us-in-your-country present. Our first thought was a book. But the old girl doesn't have an Amazon wishlist, and now that "Dick" Francis isn't writing any more, it's rather tricky. We thought we'd pop down here and pick your brains, Donnie.'

Donnie Dogs bowed again, as if this sort of thing happened most days, and let the party into his magnificently appointed emporium. He did not appear to notice the Range Rover pull away from the curb and purr down the bus lane to the corner of Duke Street where it turned left, WITHOUT INDICATING.

CHAPTER THIRTY-NINE

Hatchard's Bookstore in Piccadilly is built in the bowl of a natural volcanic amphitheatre on the confluence of no less than six organic ley lines. Its shape – four sides of roughly equal length – is said to have been copied from the peculiar earthworks in Peru, the forms of which are only truly discernible from 35,000 feet. It is said to have been the site of an ancient druidical library, but after that was burned down by inconsiderate Vikings, the store was rebuilt in 1797. The architects took their lead from the fashion of the day and included numerous mezzanine floors on different levels that can, today, be reached by stairs.

When 'Uncle' Tod Wadley, James and Emily entered the store that morning, it was a deserted arena of calm. The books were all in order, straightened and alphabetically arranged, even the photography books, which usually attracted the wrong sort of browser.

Donnie Dogs had removed his hat by this time, revealing a rippling cone of perfectly coiffed russet hair. They were making their way towards the detective fiction section when Lord Wadley gave Emily the signal. She paused and then let out a kittenish mew before keeling over. For the second time that day James Crack found himself collecting Emily's swooning form in mid-air.

'My God!' Lord Wadley cried. 'She's fainted. You couldn't get her a glass of water, could you, Donnie old chap?'

Dogs bustled away. As soon as he was gone Crack dropped Emily to the floor and both he and Lord Wadley quickly ran to the non-fiction area. Within seconds they found what they were looking for.

'Quick, James,' Wadley urged, handing the professor a ballpoint pen. 'We don't have much time.'

Crack quickly piled up all the copies of his own books on the table and began signing each one. Next to him Lord Wadley was doing the same. When they had finished they returned them to better positions of the shelf, the covers facing out, so that they were on more prominent display. By the time Donnie Dogs returned it was as if nothing had happened. Emily sipped the water and immediately felt better.

'Right,' said Lord Wadley. 'Well, now we had better buy something.'

'Why don't we just show him the barcode?' whispered Crack. 'Tell him what it is and why we need his help?'

'Are you mad?' hissed Emily. 'It will completely ruin the procedural structure of the bibliotechnical report. If you suggest that there might be an easier way to do anything – like telephone someone or do a word search on the internet – then you might as well pack up and go home before you have even begun.'

'But it will be much quicker this way. It will create a sense of urgency.'

Until that moment James Crack had never seen a Belgian woman sulk.

'All right. Do it then. But quickly,' she muttered.

Donnie Dogs had removed his apron to reveal a dark suit with which he wore a burgundy waistcoat and a blue tie. He led them to the store's main till. It was a large desk mercifully free of the usual clutter of cheap GIFT BOOKS and SPOOFS of legitimate bestsellers.

'How much do you know about barcodes?' Crack broached diffidently.

'A bit,' admitted Dogs with a wry shrug. 'What do you want to know?'

'Can your machine read this?'

Crack passed him the prolix. Dogs looked at it and sucked his teeth. Emily glanced at her watch. She had a bad feeling about this.

'What you think of as a barcode,' Donnie started,

'scholars call a UPC, or Universal Product Code. They come from a company called the Uniform Code Council, or the UCC. A manufacturer pays the UCC for a machine-readable barcode and a human-readable twelve-digit UPC number. The first six digits of the UPC number are the Manufacturer's Identification Number, or MIN. The next five digits are the item number – say a twelve-ounce can of Coca-Cola or a copy of *Harry Potter and the Half-Blood Prince*. The last digit of the UPC code is what is known as the check digit. It lets the scanner determine if it has scanned the number correctly.'

'But this,' began Emily, pointing at the barcode on the back of the prolix, 'this has no—'

But Donnie held up his hand and carried on. 'Now the check digit is calculated from the other eleven digits. One does it by adding together all the digits in the odd fields – so one, three, five and so forth – and then multiplying that number by three and adding this result to the number that one gets when one adds together all the numbers in the even fields. We'll call this result the answer number. Then one has to take whichever number it is that allows one to round one's answer number up to the nearest multiple of ten. That number then becomes the check digit.'

Lord Tod Wadley, James Crack and Agent Emily Raquin exchanged glances. 'Right,' they said.

'It sounds complicated, but the scanner performs this

calculation each time it scans an item. And there are exceptions – what we call zero suppressed numbers. Look, let me show you on this piece of paper.'

'But this one doesn't have a number!' cried Emily desperately.

'If you'll just let me finish,' Donnie continued calmly, taking a sheet of A4 paper from a block in front of him and drawing a table two columns wide and nine rows deep.

'Now the first digit of the MIN is special . . .'

Emily leaned forward across the desk and, taking her right hand back as far as it would go, she suddenly threw it forward, the fist clenched, into Donnie's chin. He staggered back a step and looked at her in surprise, then his eyes rolled into the back of his head and he folded into a heap on the floor.

'*Bravo*, Emily,' cried Lord Wadley, clapping his tiny hands together. 'Oh, *bravo!*'

CHAPTER FORTY

Jermyn Street, renowned worldwide for its exclusive gentlemen's shirt- and boot-makers, runs parallel to Piccadilly in London's St James's. It was built over the remains of what was once a women's leper colony in the Middle Ages but now it is a one-way street along its entire length, with loading bays on the north side.

It was into one of these that Alphonse Briedel steered the Range Rover. Before opening the car's door, he reached over and fumbled in the glove compartment for the FEG SMC-918, a compact pistol with great stopping power (Hungarian-made and much cheaper than the equivalent German Walther PPK, the one James Bond had used in the film *The Spy Who Loved Me*), which he tucked discreetly into the band of his suit trousers. From under his seat he removed a 12-inch 498 US Marine combat knife with a 7-inch polymer epoxy powder-coated carbon steel blade. This he hid up his sleeve.

Meanwhile, in the back of the Range Rover, Stoat had been mentally repeating the mantra of the URG since he had been bundled in to the luggage compartment in Luxembourg earlier that morning. He was by now though beginning to give up hope of ever using his legs again. The duct tape with which he had so stupidly bound and gagged himself was digging into his flesh, worse in some places than his suspenders, and it was beginning to cut off the circulation to his extremities. Corporeal mortification was beginning to set in. He knew that the next step would be gangrene.

When the boot was opened all he could see was a dark shape against the harsh light. He squinted, trying to establish the identity of the man, wondering if it was the professor. When he saw it was Wadley's manservant, Alphonse Briedel, and that he was carrying an enormously sharp knife, a surging tide of panic filled him. That he should die in the back of a car so far from Uxbridge Road was an irony over which he could not laugh. His last thoughts as Alphonse came at him were of Brown Owl.

I have failed you again, Brown Owl. This is the last time. This time I will pay for my failure with my life.

He felt the man's hands on him and the pain nearly sent him under. It grew like the molten heat of a fire, swelling and seething along his synapses, exploding in his brain. His back arched, his head was flung back in a silent scream of ecstatic agony. The ex-bookseller saw stars among the darkness and with an upwelling of grief prepared himself to welcome the release of death. Instead, he felt the duct tape being ripped from his mouth, then from the rest of his body, and this was followed by the sensation of a take-away coffee cup pressed to his lips. The taste of the liquid within reminded him first that he was alive – a riotous, joyous feeling swiftly clouded by his second thought: he did not enjoy herbal tea.

'Drink it,' murmured a deep, strongly accented male voice. 'It is a Chinese 'erbal tea made from ginkgo biloba and high potency bilberry. It is full of naturally occurring lecithin. It will help with your circulation.'

Stoat felt the warmth of the tea flood through him and where there had been pain there was now a wonderful sense of lightness. He wondered at that moment if he were dead, but when he opened his eyes at his feet he saw a pile of shredded duct tape, like the cast-off skin of a re-born snake. He looked up into Alphonse Briedel's olive-green eyes. When the Belgian smiled it was as if a light in a previously dark part of Stoat's life had been switched on at the mains. It was as if his soul were being cupped in the palm of a benign God. He forgot his pain, his fear, his abused childhood, his eerie fur that changed

CHAPTER FORTY-ONE

James Crack grasped the DataLogic handheld black plastic point-of-sale scanner in his right hand and waved its eerie red beams of light over the barcode on the back of the prolix. Lord Wadley had climbed onto a stool the better to see the results, and he and Emily were staring at the till display, their breath held in anticipation of the message. Crack had guessed that they would first be given aural confirmation that the scanner could read the barcode and then any visual data would appear on the till's customer interface.

There was a sharp electronic ping. Lord Wadley groaned in disappointment.

Crack span. 'What is it?'

'Error. Code unrecognisable. Type number manually.'

Before he had time to think about this, the front door of the bookstore burst open and the curious specimen that they had picked up at Lord Wadley's estate stood there in his rough serge suit. More than that he had a gun – the large SIG Sauer – in his left hand and he was pointing it at them.

'Get your hands up,' he growled.

The three behind the counter did as he said. The gun was held in the steady grip of someone who was clearly used to menacing others.

James Crack stared at the creature for a second. Could this be Gordon Sanitaire's assassin? Could the gun he was now wielding have fired those fatal bullets? Could this gun have even despatched the three *vacherin*? It was possible.

'What do you want?' he asked. 'We're closed.'

'I seek the *Mûre-de-Paume*, the legendary keystone.'

'Christ alive,' interjected Lord Wadley. 'Don't we all!'

'But you have it,' he snarled, waving the gun towards the diminutive lord. 'Hand it over.'

'What's the point?' asked Wadley. 'You will never be able to decipher its fiendish code.'

'Brown Owl is very clever,' answered the Stoat. 'He will be able to read it.'

'Brown Owl is very clever!' hooted Lord Wadley in mirthful derision. 'Brown Owl! What a silly name.'

The Stoat's nostrils quivered in rage. His arm shot out, aiming the heavy Swiss pistol directly at the peer's grapefruit-sized head. Wadley paled.

Just then a low groan emerged from below the sales

desk. It was Donnie Dogs. He was coming around. He rolled slowly onto his side and began to grope his way up the shelves of the desk, rubbing his jaw and making a strange hooting sound.

'Oooh-oooh! Oooh-oooh!' he moaned. 'Oooh-oooh! Oooh-oooh!'

It was as if he were imitating some kind of owl. James Crack saw the Stoat's eyes narrow in fury. They glowed bright red like the LEDs of a BMW. His knuckles whitened on the pistol grip and his long-nailed index finger flexed on the trigger. Crack tried to say something – anything – but his throat was dry and his lips were parched.

The moment Donnie Dogs poked his head above the desk the SIG Sauer exploded in Stoat's hand. The bullet clipped the veneered desk and snapped the unfortunate bookseller's head back in a cloud of blood and bone fragments. James, Emily and Lord Wadley recoiled. The erstwhile store manager's body tumbled back to the floor with a thud. A plum-coloured pool of blood began to form a foil behind his head.

'Unlucky darts,' whispered Wadley.

'No one insults Brown Owl and lives,' Stoat said. Just then the doors behind buffeted open. Alphonse burst in with the Hungarian FEG unholstered.

'Stoat? What are you doing?' he demanded of Stoat.

Lord Wadley breathed a sigh of relief, but it was

short-lived. The gun in Alphonse's hand was now pointing straight at him.

'Alphonse!' he appealed, a catch in his voice revealing his rising sense of panic. 'Kill this strange creature! Do it now.'

'Not so fast, Wadlet,' the manservant spat.

'Wadlet? That's Lord Wadley to you, Alphonse—'

'Shut up, you detestable little windbag, before I put an End to your Days 'ere and now.'

'Lawks,' murmured Wadley, visibly hurt.

'Now, bring me the prolix.'

'Why?' demanded Crack.

'No questions, you tedious, disingenuously diffident American bore.'

'Oh,' said Crack.

Emily put her hand consolingly on his shoulder.

'But it is worthless to you,' Wadley told Alphonse. 'You won't be able to find the *Mûre-de-Paume* any more than we can.'

'You,' Alphonse said, pointing the gun at Wadley, 'are coming with us. Between your pea-sized brain and the formidable intelligence of my true master, we should come up with something now that we are so close. Come on! Move it!'

With a tight nod at James and Emily, Lord Wadley slid off the chair, stepped over the dead body of Donnie Dogs and, with his tiny hands still in the air, one of them now clutching the prolix, he followed Alphonse and the Stoat to the door.

'Take me!' bellowed Crack. 'Let Lord Wadley go!'

'No chance,' cried Alphonse. 'Now lie down there and do not move or I will have no hesitation in shooting this specimen.'

He backed out of the door, pushing the diminutive lordling before him.

CHAPTER FORTY-TWO

Emily and Crack stared at each other for a few seconds in horror. Between them they had put Lord Tod Wadley in enormous danger.

The professor started for the door.

'James!' Emily cried. 'Wait!'

She was pointing at the barcode scanner, which still read: 'Error. Code unrecognisable. Type number manually.'

'We've got to do something, Emily! We can't just leave him. This Brown Owl sounds dangerous.'

'He does sound eccentrically demonic,' admitted Emily. 'But we will never catch them now and they have guns and a car. The only way to get Uncle back is to find the keystone.'

'We still need a number!'

'We don't have one. Unless . . .'

A look of revelation crossed Emily's beautiful if tired

face. She pulled from her sweater pocket a piece of paper that Crack had almost forgotten existed.

'My God,' he murmured, and not for the first time. 'The Bonifacio numbers.'

Emily swiftly crossed to the computer and carefully began typing numbers.

'He said the numbers were universal, didn't he?' she asked, realising for the first time that Donnie's barcode lecture was not just, or not only at any rate, a method of shoe-horning hard-won research into the narrative. It was vital to the progress of her bibliotechnical report.

Crack nodded.

Emily showed him the number she had typed onto the flashing field on the screen: 0552149519.

With a sense of swelling deflation, the professor quickly counted the numbers.

'But, Emily,' he said, 'there are only ten numbers. Didn't Donnie say there should be twelve, including the check digit?'

Emily sighed in despair and her head fell forward on her chest as if she were a puppet with her string cut. A tear splashed the desk before her.

'Oh James,' she murmured. 'I don't think I can go on . . .'

'But wait, Emily! What did your nephew write in the prolix?'

'He wrote "under cover" and "no marks for coming third",' she said, brought up short with hope.

'"No marks for coming third,"' said James, startled by a growing certainty. 'And didn't Donnie say something about compressed zeros before you knocked him out? No marks for coming third!'

Emily instantly understood his point.

'I will add a zero here.'

She inserted a zero in the third field.

'And there is a way to find out the last check digit. Can you remember it?'

James Crack had what his female colleagues liked to call a retentive memory. He swiftly recalled the man's words as if he had cut and pasted them from the past. Taking the piece of paper on which Donnie Dogs had started his table, Crack flipped it over and wrote a line of numbers: $0 + 0 + 2 + 4 + 5 + 9 = 20$.

'You add together the numbers in the odd fields and then multiply that by three.'

$20 \times 3 = 60$

'Then you add the result of the multiplication to the sum of the numbers in the even fields.'

$60 + 5 + 5 + 1 + 9 + 1 = 81$

'And then you need to round it up to the nearest multiple of ten, which in this case is ninety, and the difference between the two numbers – in this case nine – becomes your check digit. So the answer is nine. Of course! Nine!'

Emily was staring at him with a familiar expression of awe.

'It is just something I can do,' he said with a shrug.

Emily typed the last digit in. Her finger hovered over the return key. With the prolix and the barcode gone, this really was their only chance. She pressed return. The machine blinked. Once. Twice. And then the printer began chugging. Crack and Emily exchanged looks.

The American crossed and straightened the scroll of paper – one of them again, he thought. The printer stopped, having done its job, and the cutter slid across, neatly bisecting the sheet so that about fifteen centimetres of paper fell into Crack's outstretched hand. He read, and as he did so he shook his head and a slight smile crossed his face.

'What is it?' asked Emily.

'It's a poem,' he said simply.

CHAPTER FORTY-THREE

'Peanut?' asked Alphonse Briedel, nodding to the complimentary range of crisps and savoury snacks the Hotel Bristol offered as part of room service.

'Thanks,' replied Stoat, popping one in his mouth. 'Delicious.'

'Aren't they? I'm a bugger for anything salty, but I'm allergic to pepper.'

'Me too! We are meant for each other!' cried Stoat, girlishly. 'All Stoats are allergic to pepper. It is a rodent thing. We are missing an enzyme.'

'What do you use instead?' asked Alphonse.

'I go without,' stated Stoat, sternly.

'I use a pepper alternative called Lo-pepper™. I carry it with me wherever I go. Look.'

Alphonse removed from his jacket pocket a heavy oblong object about the size of a can of refreshing sports drink. Instead of plastic, however, it looked to be made from polished ivory or alabaster marble, mined from the hills above Sorrento, Italy, and it was ringed with dials that ran around it transversely.

'What's that?' asked Stoat.

'Lord Wadlet found it in his garden and gave it to me,' replied Alphonse as he dexterously fiddled with the dials, aligning them like a combination lock. Stoat looked on in more wonderment and he could hear Alphonse murmuring some kind of incantation under his breath. The Belgian spelled out P-E-P-P-E-R. Then he grasped either end of the device and tried to ease them apart.

'Careful, Alphonse,' he murmured to himself.

Nothing happened.

Alphonse swore quietly and then slapped his head with the heel of the palm of his hand. He began fiddling with the dials again, this time muttering P-O-I-V-R-E. Again he pulled at the ends and this time they gave. From the white of the casket slipped a jet-black, smaller version of the same thing. This was made from onyx. It had been assembled from many different pieces, however, and at its waist was a dial, not unlike those one finds on a very simple combination lock or, in fact, a pepper grinder. Alphonse shook it. There was a rattling sound. He eased the two ends apart and revealed the grinding mechanism within. Black pepper and white salt, thought Stoat. Pity there was no salt in the white bit.

With a nod of understanding Alphonse snapped the

casket shut and pocketed it carefully in the right hip pocket of his suit jacket.

'Just have to nip to the little boys' room,' he smiled, shimmying across the deep-pile carpet to the discreet door to the en-suite.

After they had left the bookstore with the prolix and Tod Wadley, Alphonse and Stoat had run down the street to the Range Rover. Once they had closed the lord in the boot and put some miles between themselves and Hatchards, they had rung Brown Owl. Stoat could remember the conversation almost exactly. He had felt a surge of triumph and then the peculiar fall at the end:

'Brown Owl! We have the *Mûre-de-Paume*, the legendary keystone!'

Brown Owl's voice was slightly muffled and he appeared to be whispering.

'That is excellent news, Stoat. You have done well.'

'And we have the very small ginger-haired scholar, too, in the boot of the car.'

Stoat was taken aback by Brown Owl's sudden whispered fury.

'And which very small ginger-haired scholar would that be?' he snapped quietly.

'The one who was with the American professor, the Belgian bibliotechnician and the *Mûre-de-Paume*,' answered Stoat.

'He is only about three feet tall and he buys his clothes

from Gap Kids,' chipped in Alphonse, who had grasped which way the conversation was going.

'He does not!' spat Brown Owl. 'Now, listen to me, Stoat, I will ring you later, but in the meantime I want you to get off the streets. Check into a hotel and lie low. But make sure it is a decent hotel with room service.'

Ordinarily the Stoat might have checked into a grimly functional budget hotel on the outskirts of town, but with Alphonse by his side, something made Stoat want to throw caution to the wind. Life was for living! *Carpe Diem!* They had immediately checked into the Hotel Bristol's famous bridal suite, renowned for its jacquard dressing gowns and discretion, and even before the porter had unloaded Lord Tod Wadley, heavily bound in duct tape, into the wardrobe in the bedroom, they had each ordered two Bellinis and half a dozen oysters from room service. In the meantime they were so gripped by a charge of excitement at having met one another that they were hardly able to stop themselves laughing. And now with Alphonse in the bathroom, Stoat sat in delighted silence for a while. Muffled thumps came from the wardrobe. Suddenly Stoat's cell phone rang. It was Brown Owl.

Stoat picked up. As Brown Owl spoke, again in the muffled tones, as if he were enclosed somewhere, Stoat could not help but glance over at the wardrobe where they had imprisoned Lord Tod Wadley. He was startled by Brown Owl's request, but he was by nature and experience inclined to obey the man who had access to VERY SECRET information and had not been wrong yet, except for a couple of times at the beginning of the evening. But that was in the past now.

'Very well, Brown Owl, I will do as you say.'

As Stoat put the phone down, Alphonse returned. He stood in the doorway of the bathroom, leaning against the jamb. Behind him Stoat could hear the running of the bath and see clouds of fragrant steam rolling through the room towards him, summoning him to oblivion.

CHAPTER FORTY-FOUR

'Emily,' said Crack with a weary sigh. 'Your nephew was a pitiless architect.'

He passed Emily the paper scroll. It was, as he had said, a poem.

> *It's not in Piccadilly where hats they doff,*
> *And if you cross one of these then you're way off.*
> *Only books, no coffee, cards, CDs or stationery,*
> *And without a chain, be very wary.*
> *It isn't the aquamarine but what shows it off*
> *Something something beef stroganoff.*
> *Ground to one and one to two but nothing up to three,*
> *That's where the Quarry you seek ought to be.*

As a bibliotechnician Emily was trained to look for themes where none existed. Jewellery, perhaps. The aquamarine, she knew, was a kind of semi-precious stone that you might hang on the end of a chain. It was not something she associated with her nephew though. But then again, as the morning wore on, it was becoming increasingly clear that she did not know her nephew at all. Emily had never read past the first page of *Larry's Party* and as for *The Stone Diaries*, they had left her cold.

. She thought back to her youth when she and Neveu had deconstructed riddles together. She would go through the text aloud and try to pick out the key meaning in each line.

'Piccadilly,' she asked now. 'What is that?'

'It's a kind of condiment, Emily, yellow and vinegary. Made from cauliflower by a company called Crosse and Blackwell.'

Emily span. Could it have been that simple? 'James! Say that again.'

Bewildered, James Crack repeated himself almost word for word. He could not share Emily's excitement.

'Well?' he asked inquisitively.

'James, you said Blackwell, *non*? Blackwell! It is the name of a famous bookstore.'

'Right,' he agreed slowly, gazing at her blankly. 'But so what?'

Emily sighed. 'James, to get anywhere in this business, you must make fabulous leaps of inference. At any moment you must be prepared to be able to connect two random objects and, even if you have to bend the facts to suit, you must wholly believe in the link you have made. If you allow any doubt to creep in you are sunk. Zis is one of zose moments.'

'So we have to get to Blackwells?'

'No!' cried Emily. 'The poem said that it – whatever it is that we seek – is not there!'

'So we have to go anywhere but Blackwells?'

'*Exactement*! Now you are getting it.'

CHAPTER FORTY-THREE

To answer the door after their bath, Alphonse Briedel tied the thick white towel around his waist and draped the jacquard robe over his shoulders. Although it was already midday, he felt no shame in still being dressed like this. It was the bridal suite after all, and he had had a long night of it.

Room service at the Hotel Bristol was swift and the Chateaubriand and Lobster thermidor 'Surf 'n' Turf' for two, the bottle of New Zealand sauvignon blanc, and the bottle of Mercurey 1996 arrived while they were in the bath. By the time they emerged, pink from the steam and their labours, the porter had laid the service on the white linen tablecloth and left the empty trolley out of the way in the corner of the room. Alphonse left a fiver on it.

'In case we're busy when he gets back,' he smiled.

'Five pounds!' admonished Stoat half jokingly.

'Who cares?' laughed Alphonse. 'We're rich. Besides, live for today for tomorrow you might die!'

They sat at the table, ravenous after their earlier efforts. Alphonse began chewing his first mouthful of steak.

'Hmph,' he muttered. 'It needs pepper.'

'Well, we did ask them not to use any,' pointed out Stoat, reasonably enough.

'You're quite right, my little dove, and that's why I love you.'

Alphonse patted Stoat's hand. It was clear to them both at that moment who was the man and who was the woman in their relationship. Both laughed. Alphonse reached across to where he had casually thrown his jacket. He took his pepper cellar from the left-hand suit pocket, held it over the food, carefully turned the white dials and let slip the black casket, then quickly twisted its dial. From within the device there was a grinding sound and from its flat bottom flakes of Lo-pepper™ drifted over his plate. He passed the grinder to Stoat.

'You know what, Stoat,' he said. 'From now on I intend to live each moment as if it were my last.'

For some reason he could not put his finger on, Stoat hesitated with the grinder hovering over the plate. Something in him shifted so subtly that he could not, even less than a second later, say exactly what it was that had happened, but he knew something unalterable had occurred that would affect his life for ever. And yet he could not say what it was. Then he also twisted the onyx ring, sending the grindings over his own plate.

Alphonse had always enjoyed wine. He began with a bracing glass of chilled New World sauvignon blanc but found it tasted . . . could it be . . . peppery? He rinsed his mouth with some of the bottled water – that also tasted odd – and then he tried the red wine. It was the same thing.

Stoat ate but watched with a growing sense of uneasy tension as Alphonse began drinking desperately at the water. His face had swollen slightly and unhealthy blotchy patches were appearing at his cheeks. His fingers, too, seemed to have lost their shape, and were turning tubular. He kept rubbing under his arms and he was becoming clumsy. He knocked the bottle of red wine over and it glugged unattended, spreading in a deep dark puddle across the white table like BLOOD. Stoat began to panic. What was wrong? What was happening to Alphonse? He could feel some kind of constriction in his own chest, and an unpleasant tightness in his skin.

'Alphonse!' he cried.

'Stoat!'

'What's happening?'

'It's the pepper!' groaned Alphonse. 'Someone switched the pepper! Oh, Jesus!'

Alphonse gripped his throat. His eyes were bulging and red, like a bull panicking before death. His voice was high and constricted now as his trachea tightened. Stoat began to feel the same panic himself. His vision swam. His hands felt two or three times their normal size.

If the pepper had been switched there could be only one man responsible. Stoat stumbled to his feet and staggered across the carpet as though he were wading through thigh-deep treacle. The room lurched. But he had to reach the wardrobe. He had to see.

'Stoat . . .' a pleading voice rose from behind. 'Please . . .'

Stoat turned. Alphonse was lying on the floor now, in some terrible calm stage, just seconds before death. He held his hand out. Stoat slowly turned and stumbled back to the only person who had ever really loved him, Alphonse Briedel. He fell to his knees by the shallow-breathing manservant and then laid himself next to his lover like a knight and his lady on a medieval tomb. He clutched the Belgian's hand in his own.

He had precious seconds of consciousness left now, but it was enough to see Lord Tod Wadley step from the wardrobe and stand at their feet, watching their last moments. Within three minutes they were dead and only then did Lord Tod Wadley turn and walk away. In his hand he held a packet of peppercorns.

*

In an office in the sprawling western reaches of London, a man replaced a telephone in its moulded plastic cradle. He sat for a moment at his desk and doodled on the blotter before him. After a minute he sat back and looked startled at what he had drawn: a stoat. A single tear rolled down his cheek.

CHAPTER FORTY-FOUR

Capitaine Georges Taureau of the TDBCFB stood in the office of Deputy Chief Inspector Justin 'Thompson' Glover, his opposite number from the Metropolitan Police based in Baker Street, the home of detection. The room might have been furnished by a Spartan, with carpet tiles on the floor and windows that gave out onto the back of another office building. A splatter of what looked like dried blood marked the grubby walls and in one corner was an iron maiden – a medieval torture device. The air was thick with the hum of outdated computer terminals.

This was an awkward interview. Capitaine Taureau did not trust his opposite number. Glover was an albino, and one of the very worst sort, with red eyes and pale skin. How he had risen so far in the police force Taureau could only speculate, although he had deduced from that peculiar handshake that it was, perhaps, either something to do with the Masons or an equal opportunity drive.

'We have reason to believe,' rumbled Taureau, 'that this American professor is armed and dangerous and at large in London. Moreover, he is accompanied by one of our own agents from the Bruxelles bibliotechnical Bureau – Agent Raquin – whom we believe has gone out of control.'

'Rogue agent, eh? Bad apple? Hmm. Licensed to kill, no doubt. A woman, too. And there's an American involved, you say? Can't have that. Any idea what they are after?'

Here Taureau paused. In truth he had no idea. He had not understood much of what had gone on that night since finding the dead body in the Grand Bibliothèque. When the death count had remained at only one body, that of the revered curator Gordon Sanitaire, Taureau had been happy to believe that James Crack had been the killer, but in the meantime four more bodies had turned up, all of them shot with the same gun and at times of the evening, according to the police pathologist, when James Crack had an unshakeable alibi. In addition, the police in Luxembourg had made some startling discoveries at Lord Tod Wadley's property. They had described them to Taureau at such great length that he had forgotten all about them. Something about a workshop? A very sophisticated radio? A wind-up microphone and a solar-panelled whatnot? Capitaine Taureau was not good with details, which was why he was so desperate to find Agent Raquin and pin the blame on her. Failing that, he was trying to work out how to implicate Lieutenant Dijon.

'No,' he admitted. 'I do not know what they are after. We lost them when they crossed the Channel. Since then, nothing.'

'We have just had a report of a shooting at a bookstore in Piccadilly. One dead. Nothing stolen. Rum, eh?'

'Rum?'

'Never mind. Do you think it might have been your man?'

Taureau shrugged.

'Problem is,' continued the unspeakably evil albino, 'that the only people seen leaving – and parking illegally, I might add – were a large rodent creature – can't be sure if it was a ferret or a stoat or even an otter, hard to tell this time of year – and a typically spineless foreign-looking man, with a moustache, described as looking like a waiter in a cheap West End musical. They left in an old Range Rover with a very small man whose head resembled an old-fashioned eighteen-panelled football. The sort they used to play with when England won the World Cup.'

'It sounds like Lord Wadley.'

'The chap from Luxembourg? Well, you had better

get down there and poke around a bit, see if you can't rustle up this American. Now look, Taureau,' Glover went on, 'I'm going to be honest with you. I have never liked Belgians. Too shifty. The Italians of the north, I call them. Criminals, every last one of them, but I hate Americans even more, so I am going to issue you with a licence to kill.'

He passed Taureau a light Heckler & Koch MP5 sub-machine-gun and a box of twenty magazines, each containing nineteen rounds of 9mm hollow-point ammunition. At that moment there was a tap on the door. It opened and Taureau leapt back, startled now, as another evil-looking albino came in. He was dressed as if for a formal police occasion in an ornate leather apron and the right leg of his trousers rolled up.

'Sir,' he said. 'We've just had a tip-off. A large stoat and an effete-looking Belgian have just checked into the Hotel Bristol. They've ordered lunch in their room.'

'Right, Capitaine,' Glover said, nodding at him significantly. 'Here's your chance to do some good, to expurgate your nation's sins. You know what to do, now go and do it.'

And Taureau knew just what to do. And he would do it.

Oh yes, he would do it all right.

CHAPTER FORTY-FIVE

Crack and Emily ran to the front door of the bookstore and spilled out onto the broad pavement just as the first patrol cars hurtled around the corner, their lights flashing and their sirens screaming. Across the street, through the swirling fog, the professor could make out a Palladian building: Burlington House, the home of the Royal Academy of Arts, founded by Sir Josephine 'Joshua' Reynolds in 1768, truly a man in touch with his Sacred Feminine side. Crack grabbed Emily and steered her over the road, through the queuing traffic and up through an old-fashioned arcade of stores.

By the time they reached Oxford Street they were utterly spent. Crack kept an eye out for any uniforms that may have followed them on foot. Emily remained fixed on the poem, trying to decipher its fiendish code.

"'If you cross one of these then you're way off,'" Emily

said aloud as they shouldered their way through the throng of tourists.

They stopped before another large bookstore as Crack checked to see if his most recent book to be published in the UK – *You've Got to Wing It to Win It!* – was prominently displayed. (It was.)

'James. What kinds of things do you cross?'

'Ts?' he suggested. 'Eyes? Fingers? Lines? Continents? I don't know. But look, Emily, Borders have got my book in the window.'

Emily gave him a tight smile. 'That's good, James. OK, so we'll leave that line. Go on to the next. "Only books, no coffee, cards, CDs or stationery."'

'Coffee!' sighed the professor. 'What a good idea.'

Emily sniffed the air. Above the stench of frying onions and diesel fumes she detected a top note of roasting beans. Her stomach rumbled and she suddenly felt exhausted. They followed the smell. It came not from a café, as they had expected, but from another bookstore. This one, however, was like no bookstore Emily had ever seen in Brussels. Instead of the relative peace of the average Belgian bookstore, undisturbed since the arrival of the Nouveau Roman, the store was buzzing with activity and noise, including a piercing percussive ping from the cash tills as the operators rang sale after sale after sale. One side of the store's boundless floor was given over to a café, while the other burgeoned with magazines. Between these wings, two escalators hummed away, taking people up to CDs, or down to videos, DVDs and computer games.

'There seems to be everything here but books,' said Emily.

'Yes, look, you can even buy pens and paper,' agreed Crack.

There was a long pause.

'James,' Emily murmured after a minute, 'if you look at the poem, almost every line tells us where we *won't* find the keystone, but in only one line does it tell us where it is. It is in whatever shows off an aquamarine.'

'We need to get on the internet,' said James.

CHAPTER FORTY-SIX

Capitaine Taureau of the TDBCFB and three detectives from SO13, the armed wing of the Metropolitan Police, crab-walked out of the elevator on the fourth floor of the Hotel Bristol. Lieutenant Dijon followed a little way behind. He had made his reservations known and was carrying only his standard-issue firearm, holstered on his hip. The first four began the slow process of covering one another with their Heckler & Koch machine pistols as they made their way up the stairs to the bridal suite on the fifth floor. It was hot work. Taureau broke a heavy sweat.

There is a standard operating procedure that law enforcement agencies the world over use for entering a room which may harbour hostile agents, but not for nothing was the motto of the TDBCFB: 'Get There First with the Most'. Even on foreign soil Taureau was not going to ask questions. He stood at the top of the stairs and directed his squad to fire at will through the door. The resulting fusillade – from the French term '*fusillade*' – lasted half an hour, during which time Taureau used all 380 rounds of his ammunition. He had thrown no less than eight stun-grenades through the hole they had blasted and he knew that the men who had abseiled off the roof had pumped a similar amount of ordnance into the room through the windows.

No one could have reasonably expected to live through that. Gun smoke hung heavily in the air. Dijon sneezed.

'I am allergic to cordite,' he explained to the English with a shrug.

Taureau discarded the Heckler & Koch and unholstered his own FN HP-SFS Hi-Power pistol – Belgian-made – that took 9mm parabellum ammunition. He approached what remained of the door warily and pushed open the top and bottom flaps. Inside was chaos. The bullets had gutted the room. Everything above two feet and below four feet had simply vanished. Lying on the floor, frosted in white dust so that they resembled marble statues of two medieval lovers, were the bodies of Stoat and Alphonse Briedel, their hands held, beatific smiles still on their faces. Taureau stepped into the room, swinging the pistol in arcs to cover any potential threat. He stood for second, legs braced. None came. He crossed swiftly and, standing over the two bodies, quickly fired a bullet into each of their foreheads – bang-bang. The dust rose, but there was little blood. It was just one of many ways to make sure they were dead.

Lieutenant Dijon and the British police officers stared at him from the doorway.

'Hardcore,' one of them muttered in admiration.

'Right. Let's search the place.'

The officers fanned out into each room. There was not much to search. With a horizontal slice taken out of the room and everywhere covered in thick plaster dust, brick chips, shrapnel and splinters, they quickly reconvened in the drawing room. All shook their heads.

'I wonder how those two died?' mused one of the English policemen, idly nodding at the two bodies.

'Suicide pact,' stated Taureau, only semi-discreetly wiping the grip of his pistol before placing it firmly in Alphonse's hand. 'Well done, men,' he said. 'Good work.'

He patted their backs as he ushered them out of the room, leaving it a devastated mess, and took the elevator down to the lobby.

'Found what you were looking for?' asked the receptionist with a bright smile.

'We are all looking for something, my child,' murmured Taureau. 'In this case it was release.'

In the fifth-floor bridal suite there was a moment of total silence until, from under the room service trolley's long skirts, a small ginger-haired man emerged clutching a battered leather book. He dusted himself down, crossed the room and relieved Alphonse of the pistol. Then he quietly left the room.

Lord Tod Wadley was alive.

CHAPTER FORTY-SEVEN

London's Charing Cross Road in the West End of England's capital city of London is the spiritual home of the British book trade. Its history goes back to the Bronze Age when, due to an administrative oversight, the houses and businesses on one side of the road became the borough of Westminster, while those on the other side remained in Camden. It is this Janus-like quality, as if the road has two faces, one facing east and the other west, which has long fascinated man. In addition the houses on one side – the left-hand side – are much lower than those on the right-hand side. This is an inside joke. The left hand is considered less deft than the right, except in left-handed people. It is a matter of historical record that almost all of the great writers – and certainly every Grand Master and each *vacherin* of the Order of Psion – were left-handed.

The road now stretches from Trafalgar Square in the

south all the way to the junction of Oxford Street and Tottenham Court Road in the north – a distance of some half a mile. When you look at it on a map it makes the shape of a quill held in someone's hand.

James Crack and Emily Raquin sat in an internet café on the street, looking across at Borders bookstore, waiting for their browser to boot up. When it had, James Crack started typing: 'What shows off an aqua-marine.'

He pressed enter and within 0.61 seconds Google came back with 26,901 results, of which 1–50 showed up on the screen in front of him. Impressive, thought Crack. But his search was too broad. He added quotation marks at each end and tried again.

Only one answer. He clicked the link.

It was an obscure would-be author's website. Toni Lemmons. Who the hell is Toni Lemmons? wondered Crack. There was some text concerning a novel that he was writing, a few reviews he had done for a right-wing newspaper and, on the home page, a photo showing a fat-faced, bespectacled man with short hair sitting at his computer.

He had the face he deserved, thought Emily, peering over Crack's shoulder. He has never known a day without red wine. He has been lucky all his life.

It was not clear where the aquamarine reference occurred on the site, and there was no internal search

engine. Crack scrolled through the samples of work,
using the web search on each page until he found it.
Just one sentence in the middle of a sample chapter.
Could Gordon Sanitaire have done this exact same
thing?

The chapter concerned two South African jewellers
selling a ring to a young couple. The ring, as even
James's first reading could determine, would turn out
to be haunted by some kind of malignant ghost. It was
a silver ring that held a large aquamarine and in a frag-
ment of poorly realised dialogue one of the jewellers –
a man named Ralph – was extolling the virtues of the
stone.

'You see, *what shows off an aquamarine* so beautifully is
a silver foil like this beautiful clasp.'

A silver foil? What the hell did that mean? Crack put
his head in his hand, trying to think, and glanced down
the length of Charing Cross Road towards Trafalgar
Square, when suddenly it hit him like a bolt of ball light-
ning in the rotating drum of a washing machine. It was
right there in front of him.

'Emily!' he hissed urgently. 'Do you suppose your
nephew's lines could be referring to bookstores? Didn't
you say Blackwells was a bookstore?'

Emily looked startled. She fluttered her eyelashes. 'It
is possible, of course,' she murmured. 'My nephew loved
bookstores.'

'Then look over there,' Crack said with a quiet smile.

Emily followed his pointing finger to where, about a hundred feet away, a sign read 'Waterstone's'.

'Waterstone's,' she murmured, feeling that familiar sense of wonderment rise within her again. 'Aquamarine!'

While Emily stared across the road James read the line of sublime poetry to her again.

'"It isn't the Aquamarine, but what shows it off."'

'So it is not Waterstone's?' asked Emily bleakly, awash with misery again.

'Of course,' admitted James, 'your nephew might not have meant bookstores at all. He—'

'James,' interrupted Emily sharply. 'If you are going to suggest any alternative possibilities, I must stop you now. That is a schoolboy error. In any bibliotechnical report it is essential the principals believe, and are seen to believe, the central premise. If they don't, then the whole thing becomes incredible and it falls apart.'

Crack thought for a second. 'Emily, it sounds as if you have swallowed the *Mûre-de-Paume*; you seem to know so much about compiling bibliotechnical reports, you could write the Asti Spumante Code.'

Emily was about to speak, but dropped her eyes at the last minute. It seemed a dangerous thing to say aloud. She suddenly felt her nephew by her shoulder again.

Suddenly she gasped aloud. A foil showed off the Aquamarine. A foil.

CHAPTER FORTY-EIGHT

Capitaine Taureau snapped his cell phone shut and took a long draught from a pint of Guinness. On the desk in front of him, his steak and kidney pie with extra mash and onion gravy was slowly cooling. Taureau had begun to see that there might be some fall-out from the incident at the Hotel Bristol. A chambermaid had gone up to change the sheets and had fainted. Two bodies had been found with identical bullet holes in their foreheads and the room had been left a shambles. The *London Evening Standard* was calling it a bloodbath and the TV news teams had seized on some rumours of an execution. But there was no mention of the pistol that he had pressed into Stoat's hand. Now what had become of that?

Glover had come in and was pacing the room nervously, his evil red eyes glowing in the early afternoon gloom, his bloodlust all too evident. In another office, his men were running the CCTV images from all the cameras in central London through the Face Recognition Technology (FERET) programme. If Crack or Emily appeared on CCTV, Baker Street would soon know.

'All we can do is wait. Don't like it. Want to get out there and get stuck in. Can't be dealing with going through all this CCTV footage.'

'They will turn up eventually,' growled Taureau, picking up the machine pistol. 'And when they do . . .' He cocked the Heckler & Koch ominously. It was a crisp, threatening sound.

'So who stole that gun, eh? Not the chambermaid. Still unconscious. Shock. Hah. Means someone was either there when it happened—'

'Impossible!' interrupted Taureau bullishly. 'No one could have lived through that.'

'Then they must have been there shortly afterwards. Why didn't they call the police?'

Taureau shrugged. He had been awake too long now to think very much about peripherals. He wanted only to find that American and when he found him he was going to kill him.

'Must be someone else after your American, too. Any ideas?'

For an albino, Glover was quick. Taureau had not considered making this outrageous inference, but it made some sense. The only problem was, who could it be? Had he lost sight of anyone? He ticked off the characters

in the plot one by one. All accounted for except . . .
And then it hit him with all the force of a wicker carpet-
beater. Lord Tod Wadley. Where was he?

'Detective Inspector!' snorted Taureau in triumph.
'Put an all-points bulletin out on a three-foot ginger-
haired aristocrat with a head like an old-fashioned
mini-football. His name is Lord Tod Wadley and he is
armed with an FN HP-SFS Hi-Power sidearm, although
he will have some difficulty using it, he is so pathetically
small.'

Glover made the call and was already strapping on a
flak jacket with a machete holster on the back when the
phone on his desk rang. He snatched it up.

'Glover here. Good. They're *where*?'

After a second he put the phone down, a puzzled
expression on his pallid face.

'Most extraordinary thing. They're in a bookstore.'

CHAPTER FORTY-NINE

Emily Raquin and James Crack crossed Manette Street, unaware that their image had been picked up by a CCTV camera protruding from a ledge on the corner of the next-door office block. They entered W&G Foyle's famous bookstore via the side door and stopped for a second to assess the task ahead. If Charing Cross Road was the heart of the British book trade, then Foyles was its beating epicentre. Could the *Mûre-de-Paume*, the legendary keystone, really be hidden in this building? And if so, where? There were more than five million books on show on at least thirteen miles of shelves.

'*Mon Dieu,*' said Emily. 'It could be anywhere.'

It certainly looked chaotic, but James Crack was constantly surprised by how many people thought that trying to find a book in Foyles was difficult or the lay-out a mystery. *No mystery at all*, he thought. *No mystery at all.* The ground floor is given over to fiction, with the books on shelves with their spines showing outward. Other types of books, including his own works, were on other floors. The administrative offices were on the fifth floor, reached by tight stone steps or the new lifts, and deliveries came through the back door. The post was picked up from dispatch in the basement.

Gilbert and George Foyle, both sadly dead now, had been brothers since their birth in 1903 and together they had opened a bookstore on the corner of Charing Cross Road selling textbooks. Although not much had changed during the first century of its existence, the beginning of its second century as an independent family-run bookstore ushered in a new generation of owners and in recent months the store had undergone a top-to-toe transformation. All the building work had been done by hand, of course, including the fitting of a new piranha tank in the children's department.

'James,' Emily was saying as she surveyed the men and women – boys and girls really, thought Crack, just kids – who were manning the fiction desk. 'I am impressed by your confidence that something you found on the internet is the key to the Asti Spumante Code.'

'It might not be the key, Emily, but it is definitely the next step along. We still have the last three lines of the poem to decipher, remember.'

Emily looked down at the poem.

Something something beef stroganoff.
Ground to one and one to two but nothing up to three,
That's where the Quarry you seek ought to be.

'My nephew was a vegetarian,' Emily said. 'Why would he mention stroganoff, which is a meat-based dish, *non?*'

Crack nodded. As Catt Butt Professor of Para-literal Meta-symbolist Studies and author of numerous works on the subject, he was often amazed by how few people knew that beef stroganoff – a combination of beef, mushrooms and sour cream – was the prize-winning recipe of a cooking competition held in the 1890s in Russia's St Petersburg. The chef who devised the recipe worked for Pavel Alexandrovich Stroganov, a member of one of Russia's grandest noble families. Why the letter 'v' at the end had changed to a double 'f' was one of para-literalism's most elusive mysteries.

'Anything that looks out of place, James, must convey a message,' stated Emily firmly.

Crack stopped and stared at her. That is very good, I must try to remember that, he thought.

'But what?' she went on. 'The beef stroganoff line tells us little or nothing – perhaps it is merely padding? To make a rhyme with doff and off?'

'It is possible,' agreed Crack.

'James,' said Emily after a while staring at the lines,

making less and less sense of them as time passed, 'there is a technique practised in bibliotechnography that we call the sucker punch and I think this might be the time to use it.'

'Oh yes?' he stated neutrally.

His eye was already roving over the next line. He heard the words that came next as if they had been spoken a long distance away, and a long time ago. The strange thing was, however, that he could almost have said that he knew they were coming.

'I think you should ask someone,' Emily said.

James instantly broke a light sweat. He stepped back. He knew this scene had been played out a million times in a million different places by a million different people. It did not make it any better. He felt trapped by its inevitability.

'Ask someone what?' he mumbled as absently as he could manage, running his finger over the next line of poetry. Look busy, James, he told himself. Look busy and she'll give up and go and ask someone herself.

'Ask someone what they make of this line – they might know the store. It might ring a bell with them.'

'Wait a second. Ground. Ground to one. What's ground? Ground beef? Ground beef! Emily!'

Emily stared hard at him for a second. During that long moment, Crack wondered if over the course of the twelve hours her face had become somewhat less soft.

She snatched the paper from his hand and approached the desk. A young man with floppy blond hair and heavy horn-rimmed glasses stopped his game of computer chess long enough to glance up at her.

'Yeah?' he asked.

'Does this mean anything to you?' she asked and read out the line of poetry. 'Ground to one and one to two but nothing up to three.'

'Is it fiction?' he asked in a sing-song London accent.

'No,' said Emily, briefly taken aback. 'It is poetry.'

'Third floor, then.'

He was back to his game before Emily had time to draw the breath for another question.

CHAPTER FIFTY

The members of SO13 were hand-picked from police forces all over Britain to make an elite rapid-response quick-reaction force that could, day or night, get to any part of London at a second's notice. From the moment the call went out from the situation room in the basement of their headquarters in Baker Street at two o'clock, the thirty-three men of Q Brigade – all of them fully albino and unspeakably evil – moved like a well-oiled machine. They reached Tottenham Court Road at three o'clock and had Foyles completely surrounded less than an hour later.

Capitaine Georges Taureau and Lieutenant Jacques Dijon, officially seconded from the Belgian police, stood with Detective Inspector Glover in the very same internet café that James and Emily had vacated only minutes before. They were watching as the regular police blocked off the surrounding roads and evacuated the nearby

buildings. Within minutes Foyles was completely iso-
lated.

'Going smoothly,' murmured Glover, peering through
an ANVS-1330 night-vision monocular. He was wearing
the famous black boiler-suit uniform of SO13 and carrying the standard-issue Colt SR16 M4 assault rifle with
attached grenade launcher on a strap over his shoulder.
On his hip he had a 9mm Sigma SW40F pistol, complete
with a silencer and red-dot scope. As an officer he was
entitled to carry a sword (and grow a beard) and so he
also had his samurai sword strapped to his waist and the
machete on his back.

He held a radio to his mouth and was about to
murmur a command into it when he stopped, startled.
He lowered the radio.

'Well, well. Whatever next,' he murmured to
Taureau. 'Wonder how he got through the blockade.'

Taureau and Dijon, carrying only their sidearms,
craned forward. When they saw what Glover was pointing at, they too were suddenly overcome by waves of
apprehension. Along the pavement hurried the unmis-
takable figure of Lord Tod Wadley, his dressing gown
flapping behind him.

'Explains your gun, anyway,' said Glover, nodding at
the diminutive aristocrat.

Lord Tod Wadley was carrying the big Belgian pistol
in both hands and before any of the insidiously evil albi-

nos of SO13 could stop and shoot him he had raced across Manette Street and disappeared into the bookshop.

'How did he know where to find Raquin and Crack?' asked Dijon.

Taureau looked briefly uncomfortable. 'Police radio?'

'What now, hmm?' asked Glover rhetorically.

'Let us wait a second,' cautioned Taureau. 'We will see what happens.'

'Think I'll get my chaps to move a little closer, all the same,' demurred Glover, and then snapped 'standby' into the radio.

Dijon watched aghast as fifteen fully armed albino operatives of A Section, Q Brigade, SO13 sprinted across the tarmac and threw themselves against the walls on either side of the store's boundless windows. From the parapet at the top of the building fifteen long coils of hi-spec nylon rope came looping down, followed immediately afterward by fifteen albino operatives of B Section, Q Brigade, SO13, their bandoliers, Dijon could see even from this distance, groaning with M67 fragmentation hand grenades.

He sensed trouble.

CHAPTER FIFTY-ONE

The escalators at Foyles extend only as far as the second floor. The reason for this is lost in the mists of time, but Grail historians believe that Christina Foyle, the niece of the founders, and a woman with a trenchant belief system, would tolerate no change in its medieval layout or operations systems. Sometime in the 1970s she took a vacation and while she was away, a relative, who was someone with a future interest in the store, had the escalators installed and intended them to reach the fourth floor. Christina heard about this, cut her holiday short, and came home like an Assyrian on the fold to stop the work in its tracks. The unknown relative was never seen again.

When James Crack and Emily Raquin reached the second floor of the bookstore by escalator they stood for a second in confusion. Where was the next set that would lead them up to the third floor?

Typical British, thought Crack. No escalator. They've got one from the ground floor to the first floor and one from the first floor to the second floor but not up to the third. He stopped for a second. Now why did that sound familiar?

There seemed to be nobody around to ask where they should go. Ahead of them was the art department and beyond that, clearly a dead end. Emily strode forward and turned left into a bright-looking passage between two ornately carved pillars.

What she saw disappointed her.

She was standing in a small side gallery. It was a medium-sized room – about eighteen metres long and six metres wide. Along the top of one wall was a line of windows that gave out onto a redbrick building and above that she could make out the grey London sky. It was what was hanging on the walls of the room that had amazed her, an exhibition of art by a man named C. Reginald Dalby.

When Crack followed her into the room, his mind was already playing with half-remembered echoes of words he could not quite recall. He took one glance at the paintings and stopped in his tracks. He broke a heavy sweat and his hair stood on end. Thomas the Tank Engine! The professor's mind span back over the events of the past night, back to the Grand Bibliothèque. Of course! The book that Gordon Sanitaire had been

clutching to his dead body had been *Troublesome Engines,*
by the Reverend Awdry, illustrated by C. Reginald Dalby.
But where was the link? What had the two in common?

All the pictures – and there were about twenty of
them – were of Thomas the Tank Engine and his friends;
mostly other steam engines, but also, he noted, a bus.

When Crack explained how he had found Reverend
Awdry's book clutched in the arms of Sanitaire, Emily
understood that the code had been designed to lead them
to this room.

'The answer must be here, James,' she murmured,
almost overwhelmed by the upwelling of wonderment. 'I
feel it.'

'I know the Reverend Awdry was a member of the
Order of Psion,' murmured Crack, temporarily baffled,
'but I didn't know that he was at all senior. I didn't think
your nephew would have known him.'

'But if not then why send us here?' she asked.

'To make a colossal leap of inference?' he asked with
one of his quiet smiles.

Emily looked at the professor again, almost unable to
speak. She knew now why her nephew had tried to
connect them, why, indeed, he said he loved James
Crack.

'Exactly, James,' she whispered. 'That's exactly why
we are here.'

'And I think I can help, Emily,' said Crack. 'Look.'

He was pointing over her shoulder at one of the paintings. It was of a train idling in a quarry. Next to the
painting was a small square of plastic bearing the legend:
'*The Quarry* by C. Reginald Dalby (1954).'

CHAPTER FIFTY-TWO

At first glance *The Quarry* was an unexceptional painting. It looked to be about eighty by sixty centimetres and was enclosed in a simple rosewood frame. It showed a blue steam engine idling in a quarry while men in blue railway uniforms coupled various brown – presumably wooden? – trucks to its tender. But what set this painting apart was that the engine, instead of a face, had a slither of reflective glass in its place. A mirror.

The pair were approaching the painting when they heard a familiar voice behind them. They span.

Lord Tod Wadley entered the gallery with a tight smile on his leathery face and a huge Belgian-made pistol clutched in his teeny-weeny hands.

'Hullo, you two,' he said jauntily. 'I hoped I'd find you here.'

'Uncle,' cried Crack, making to hug the Briton. 'Just in time! How did you get away?'

'Oh, nothing to it,' he shrugged, putting the heavy pistol on the desk. 'Just had to pick my moment. Have you found the *Mûre-de-Paume*? The legendary keystone?'

Crack and Emily turned to look at the painting.

'It has to be something to do with this picture,' said Crack, indicating the painting before them.

'My God!' cried Wadley, leaping back. '*The Quarry*! Of course. Of course! Why didn't I think of it?'

Shock drained the blood from his dubbined face, leaving him temporarily speechless. He opened his mouth, gaping at Emily and Crack for a few seconds.

'Uncle? Are you all right?'

'All this time,' Wadley managed to squeak. 'All this time and it was right in front of our eyes.'

'The painting?' asked Emily.

Lord Wadley shook his head to clear his thoughts and then turned and stood before the painting, looking up at it.

Crack and Emily had assumed *The Quarry* was just an oddity included by the exhibition's curator for the entertainment of children who might want to know what they would look like if they were one of Reverend Awdry's steam trains. The more Crack looked at it, however, the less likely that became. It hung at about five feet high on the wall, for a start, high above Lord Tod Wadley or, for that matter, any child who might be interested.

'This painting, my dear,' stated Lord Wadley, now looking at Emily in a strange manner, 'is the key to finding the *Mûre-de-Paume*. You see, Wilbert Awdry and his illustrator C. Reginald Dalby enjoyed a famously tempestuous relationship. It's well documented in Psion literature and most of it points to artistic differences as being the cause of their notorious split in 1956.

'Now, Awdry was a member of the Order at a very low level, but Dalby was one of the three *vacherin* before an untimely death when a bookshelf collapsed on her while she was giving a reading at the Edinburgh Festival.'

At first Emily had been pleased to see Lord Wadley safe and sound but now she was not so sure. She felt a familiar wave sweep through her. 'Go on,' she muttered between clenched teeth.

'Psion scholars always believed that the schism between Dalby and Awdry was brought about by Dalby wanting to anthropomorphise the trains, to make them human, you understand? So that their personal relationships took centre stage. Awdry on the other hand championed all those dry, railway-related plots. This is why the engines' faces became bolder and more expressive as the plots grew steadily more Byzantine.'

'Uncle, this is all very fascinating, but what has it to do with the *Mûre-de-Paume*?'

'The legendary keystone? At first glance almost nothing, but this painting – sometimes called the painting of puzzles – was only found in an attic in 1978 and since then academics have argued ceaselessly about what it means. With your assistance, my dear James, my dear Emily, I think I may have just deciphered it. It is clear that it is a message from Dalby. One which if I had listened to earlier might have saved a devil of a lot of bother.'

Well?

'What Dalby is telling us here,' said Wadley with the air of a conjuror pulling a rabbit from a hat, 'is that objects are not always just objects. Or to put it another way, things which we think of as objects sometimes turn out to be something quite different.'

'So it's another one of Dalby's anthropomorphisms?' asked Emily.

'Not quite. One of the painting's most singular aspects is that if James or I were to look into the mirror, we would get little or no idea of what we might look like as a train. Try it, James.'

Crack approached the painting and bent his knees to peer into the face of the nameless steam train. The mirror was not round or elliptic as one might expect, but was ragged, as if shadows were falling over it, perhaps from the quarry cliff face. He bobbed his head to get a better view, but no. As Lord Wadley had suggested, he could not see his face properly in the mirror. When he stepped back he still had no idea what he would look like as a train.

'No luck? Not surprising. No one looks like a train

when they look into the mirror, you see. Mainstream academics have put this down to a failure of execution – that Dalby simply wasn't good enough – while Psion scholars have always known that it was a code.'

'But a code to what?' asked Emily.

'Good question. A code to a face. I believe this mirror will work only for a certain face. The face of the *Mûre-de-Paume* . . .'

'The *Mûre-de-Paume* has a *face*?' Crack asked incredulously.

'Indeed, yes, James. That is what Dalby is trying to tell us. Now Emily, my dear, indulge me, if you will, and have a look for yourself. If I am right, I think we are in for something of a surprise.'

Emily approached. The painting was hung at a perfect height for her to look into the face of the anonymous steam engine. She stared at the mirror for a long moment without moving and then Crack saw the blood drain from her face.

She stepped back sharply. She felt her throat tighten and the skin on her scalp prickle.

'Emily? Are you all right,' asked Crack, solicitously.

Emily turned to him, her face now deathly white. When she had looked in the mirror, she had seen, instantly, a perfect image of herself as a steam train. Her face fit the mirror. She was the *Mûre-de-Paume*. Emily was the legendary keystone.

CHAPTER FIFTY-THREE

For a moment the three of them stood there, too stunned to speak. Then Lord Tod Wadley seemed to gather himself.

'Oh dear, what a pity,' he said with a false note in his voice that made James Crack spin on his feet. He found himself face to face with the muzzle of a large foreign-looking pistol.

'Not so fast, if you don't mind, old boy.'

Crack broke sweat again. 'Uncle, what's wrong?' he stammered. 'I don't understand.'

'No. You never do, do you, James? Never mind. Where you are going you won't have to do much thinking. I am sorry for you, Emily. I have enjoyed our little outing and you are a game gal, but all good things must come to an end. I had hoped to be able to end this without any more bloodshed, but you must see my position.'

'What position is that?' Crack asked, genuinely perplexed.

'Did I not explain? I am after the Asti Spumante Code, James, and I mean to have it by the end of the day.'

'But aren't we all looking for the Asti Spumante Code? I thought that is what we had been doing all day?'

'Yes. You are right. We have. But for different reasons. Anyway, James, I don't have time for all this. I must be off. Emily, you are coming with me. We have some business to attend to. James, old boy, it has been rich and rare, and I hate to have the death of another innocent on my hands but here goes . . .'

'What do you mean another innocent?' snapped Crack.

'Playing for time, James, eh? Well, all right, I've got five minutes.'

'Who else have you killed?'

'Tonight or ever?'

'Start with ever.'

'Oh well, it began a while back. I am sorry for having to kill your poor grandfather, Emily, and your grandmother, come to that, and your father, mother, four aunts, five uncles and brother.'

'But they died in an accident.'

'Nope,' said Lord Wadley with a hint of smugness that James Crack found repellent. 'All murdered on my orders. An old mobile library truck forced their bus off the road when they were on some damn fool PEN trip to Eastern Europe.'

'It was an accident!' cried Emily, stunned.

'Very well, have it your own way,' chuckled Wadley. 'Just as that little shooting in the Grand Bibliothèque last night was an accident.'

'You killed my nephew?'

'I had a man take care of it. Well, a stoat, actually. Cheaper.'

'But why, Uncle?' demanded Crack incredulously. 'Why d'you do it?'

'Simple. As I said, I'm after the Asti Spumante Code.'

'You want it so bad you would kill for it?'

'Well, as you Americans would say: duh!'

'But how would killing my family help you get it?'

'Ah, of course, I am forgetting. Emily, you don't know who they were, do you?'

'My parents? *Non.*'

Emily had a vague recollection of a white beard and soft, fragrant arms, but that was it.

'Your mother, Emily, was Ernest Hemingway. Your father was Scott Fitzgerald.'

'But then . . .' started Crack, staring at Emily. 'That makes you . . .'

'Exactly, James,' broke in Wadley. 'I did not believe it before tonight, but it seems Emily is the next in line to become the Grand Master of the Order of Psion, and the next person to hold the secret of the Asti Spumante Code.'

Crack broke more sweat. Emily trembled.

'I will never help you,' she said defiantly. 'You killed my family!'

'As well as heartbreak, Emily', said Wadley, 'all good authors know their share of pain. I will torture you until you write the book I want. Quite simple really.'

'You are an animal Wadley! And to think I used to think of you as a friend.'

'I don't think you quite understand the power of the Asti Spumante Code, James. Once I have it I will have such power over the publishing industry they will do everything I want. All those tiresome little independent publishers producing those exquisite little hardbacks will be history. They will become part of my conglomerate. Everything will be in paperback. I will decide who reads what, when and where. The threat of the Asti Spumante Code has hung over us far too long. I will even be able to get the big bookshops to categorise their books as dick-lit and chick-lit. If I possess the Asti Spumante Code I can ensure that men will read thrillers for ever and women frightful codswallop about girls in their twenties who think they have it all . . .'

'You are evil!' cried Emily, suddenly springing to her feet and launching herself at him.

Wadley span. The gun exploded. The bullet crashed

past her, just missing her left shoulder and embedding itself into one of the priceless train pictures. The slim bibliotechnician was lithe enough to knock the little man to the ground, but he still had the gun.

Crack lunged and caught the peer's wrist, knocking the gun high into the air. Emily cat-rolled and caught it before it hit the ground, and she was on her knees, pointing it at Wadley's head, before he could move a muscle.

But something was wrong.

Both Crack and Emily reeled back in horror.

Lord Tod Wadley had literally come apart. His limbs lay at impossible angles, his head had come away from his neck and it lolled grotesquely. But instead of blood, the only things that trickled from Lord Tod Wadley were a plume of smoke from a sparking electrical connection and a little sawdust from a small vent in his cheek.

He was a puppet, a radio-controlled mannequin, a robot.

The question they now had to ask themselves was: whose robot was he?

CHAPTER FIFTY-FOUR

The first sign of the attack came with a shower of breaking glass as the officers of SO13 broke the ground-floor windows and doors of Foyles and threw in a volley of powerful stun grenades. These 'flash and bang' grenades are intended to provide a non-lethal method of neutralising and disorienting enemy personnel. Their explosions and blinding flashes reverberated through the building, terrifying customers and staff alike. Many fell to their faces, convinced they were going to die. Most of them were right.

Meanwhile the policemen suspended from the temporary anchors on the roof of the building had gained access to the fourth floor through the windows and down the stairs from the administrative offices on the fifth floor. They had any staff and customers who remained alive pinned into the complimentary philosophy section and had unleashed a murderous arc of fire to clear the rest of the floor. In this way the music, health and well-being, humanities and learning sections were all more or less vaporised. No one was left standing as SO13 cleared the floors department by department, rigorously following the drills that Glover had drummed into them. First five or six MK3A2 concussion offensive hand grenades, then the murderous volleys of small arms machine-gun fire, then the shouted warnings.

From his position in the internet café across the street, Detective Inspector Glover monitored his men's progress with some satisfaction. He watched as A Section secured the ground floor and B Section took the fourth floor, smiling and nodding to himself as the windows of both floors started billowing black smoke, marking the passage of his crack albino policemen. Through the clouds he could see the bright flashes of exploding ordnance. Then, while the fourth floor caught fire, the first and third floors started filling with the black smoke, too. It was on the second floor that the trouble really started.

The fifteen officers of A Section who had gone in on the ground floor had encountered no resistance there or on the first floor. B Section reported the same situation on the fourth and third floors. Both, however, met increasingly heavy resistance on the second floor, where the enemy seemed numerous, well armed and well drilled. The tell-tale rattle of short bursts of gunfire meant that whoever was in there knew what they were doing.

The fire-fight intensified as B Section tried to flank the insurgents at the same time that A Section opted for a full-out attack with incendiary hand grenades. Casualties among the SO13 officers were well into double figures when Detective Inspector Glover called on the snipers he had positioned on the parapets of the nearby buildings to provide indiscriminate suppressing fire through the second-floor windows of the bookstore. He himself took up position on the corner of Manette Street and brought his grenade-launcher to bear. Within thirty seconds the whole shop was on fire from top to bottom and it was soon clear that no one would get out alive.

CHAPTER FIFTY-FIVE

James Crack and Emily Raquin did not have enough time to think about Lord Tod Wadley before a series of huge explosions rocked the building. They were instantly thrown to the ground. A deafening boom reached them along with a rolling cloud of gagging smoke. Plaster dust fell from the ceiling above. It was almost impossible to see anything and all around them they could hear the staccato rattle of machine-gun fire. Ricocheting bullets and deadly shards of shrapnel whistled and snapped in the air around their ears.

'Emily!' Crack bellowed, his ears ringing. 'Emily! Are you all right?'

Emily had been thrown face down and she was now lying on her stomach, staring at Tod Wadley's body, a scant foot from her face. It had been torn open by some splinter and the lights of a complicated computer were flashing yellow and green. It kept making an incomprehensible noise. The right hand was twitching in a grotesque impression of life.

'Emily!' Crack tried again 'Emily! We've got to get out of here.'

'Wait!' cried Emily. She reached forward and carefully removed the prolix from Wadley's dressing-gown pocket.

Crack staggered to his feet and tried to make his way towards her as another explosion ripped through the building. It sent him flying against the far wall. Beyond the gallery, he could hear the bookshelves falling one after another, like dominoes. Men and women were screaming now. Gunfire continued – short, sharp, deadly bursts followed by deafening explosions and the sound of running feet. Another blast. The ground seemed to jump and tip. Crack tripped and fell. A stabbing lick of flame shot through the window above him, into the space he had vacated. It would have incinerated him instantly. Instead three of Dalby's priceless paintings caught fire, the oil paint burning with an acrid, throat-catching cloud of greasy black smoke.

He took Emily's hand and pulled her away from Wadley's body, dragging her towards the pillars of the gallery. Beyond lay carnage. Although a single sheet of paper burns easily enough at comparatively low temperatures, when these sheets are bound together to form a book, they will only burn at Fahrenheit 400. The lack of oxygen will often put the fire out before the book is destroyed. Which is why the insanely evil operatives of SO13 were equipped with AN-M14 TH3 incendiary hand grenades, full of a thermate mixture that is designed to burn at temperatures of up to 4,000°F and converts itself into molten iron. It does not need oxygen and can burn underwater. The second floor had been turned into a fire-storm, sucking the oxygen through the windows and roasting the bodies that lay around the anthropology section. One or two members of staff were vainly attempting to tackle the fire with some fire extinguishers, a bucket of sand and an old jumper soaked in water. A burst of well-aimed tracer rounds cut them down as a scythe might hack through a nettle patch.

There was only one way out. Crack grabbed Emily and forced her head down behind the fallen shelves. He pushed her from behind.

'Come on. Leave them. This way,' he bellowed in her ear. 'It's our only chance!'

He forced her back through the art department towards the doors to the emergency fire escape. The flames were irrelevant now; it was the lack of oxygen that would kill them. Or the 9mm bullets that thudded into the walls and the shelves around them.

'Keep low!' shouted Crack, his voice harsh now. Emily held her sweater over her face as a mask against the toxic fumes. They ran to the doors and forced them open, letting in more oxygen. Behind them the fire roared its approval. Crack turned and slammed the doors shut, scalding the palms of his hands as he did so.

They were on the stone landing of an echoing flight of stairs. An old iron banister led them down but they could tell by the smoke that snaked its way from below that the fire had caught fast on the ground or the first floor. The only way was up.

'Come on! Quick!'

Crack set off, dragging Emily behind him up the stairs. The higher they got the cooler it became and soon they burst through a set of doors and emerged onto an iron fire-escape, a walkway that led towards the rear of the burning bookstore, to where it joined the houses on Greek Street.

'This way!' shouted Crack.

They sprinted along the fire-escape, their footsteps unheard among the explosions and the roar of the fire. An SO13 sniper saw them from the building opposite and opened up on them with his M16 assault rifle. James and Emily flung themselves down as the bullets pecked their way over them, smashing into the roof tiles and covering their backs with slate splinters. They waited until the marksman stopped to change his magazine and then they were up again. Safety lay in a glazed doorway ten yards away. They reached it just as the gunfire started again, pulverising the door above their heads as once again they threw themselves down and through the now open doorway.

They found themselves lying on deep-pile carpet, albeit that it was covered in broken glass and the splinters from the destroyed door. On hands and knees they made their way through into another room and it was as if they had entered into another world.

CHAPTER FIFTY-SIX

The first thing that James Crack saw when he raised his eyes from the carpet was a concert grand piano, which stood foursquare in the corner of a boundlessly large salon. The professor got cautiously to his feet and helped Emily do the same. They looked about them. The room was deserted. The noise of the gunfire and explosions had abated somewhat and all that could be heard was the sound of a mahogany grandfather clock ticking sonorously against the far wall. Wells of bright sunlight fell from the floor-to-ceiling windows along all three of the walls and it became clear that they were in the penthouse. Over the fire, mercifully not lit today, there was a marble chimneypiece covered with silver-framed photographs, a cut-glass vase of perfectly poised tulips, and a long oil painting of the famous female impersonator Danny La Rue.

'James,' murmured Emily, wiping a smut of sooty

carbon from her cheek, 'I have been here before. A long time ago, I can 'ardly remember it.'

Crack walked around the broad sofas and armchairs and approached the chimneypiece. One of the photos had caught his eye.

'It is not a happy memory,' Emily continued slowly.

'Could it have been something to do with this?' Crack asked. He turned and held one of the photographs. Its frame was of polished wood and simply made. A carpenter's frame, he thought. The picture, an old black-and-white snap, was of Carol Shields dressed in what Crack could only describe as a dirndl. On her head she wore a wig of long silver hair tied in plaits. Next to her stood a figure that James recognised all too clearly.

The beautiful bibliotechnician sobbed sharply when she saw the photo.

'Neveu!' she cried out.

'Emily,' Crack said, 'let me guess. This is why you fell out with your nephew all those years ago?'

Emily nodded.

She could remember coming to this strange place soon after her parents had died in that car crash. She had been put to bed in one of the rooms towards the back of the apartment, but something had woken her in the night – a noise with which she was not familiar. She came to find her nephew and opened the door to the salon to find music playing. And then she saw him. He was dancing on a makeshift stage in a line with his arms around the shoulders of two other men, one on each side. They were all wearing short frilly dresses and fish-net stockings, and they were dancing a strange dance. They kept kicking their legs in the air and before them a man in a silk dressing gown and a silver-topped stick was beating out a rhythm and crying 'oop la!' every time they advanced to the front of the stage.

Crack sighed as she related the tale. All those wasted years when you could have been friends, he thought.

'Emily,' he said. 'What you witnessed was something called "hetero-games".'

''Etero-games?'

'Yes. You see, Emily, many men like to dress up as women and enact what they call "revues", but it does not mean that your nephew was a sex-mad pervert. Quite the opposite, in fact.'

'But my nephew was a woman.'

'One of the lucky ones,' said James. 'But she was good to the rest of us, showed us the way it should be done.'

'Right,' said Emily doubtfully. 'So it was not unusual?'

'Not at all,' explained Crack. 'It is a way of achieving spiritual enlightenment. You see, for those of us who cannot ever become members of the Order of Psion, who can never achieve the Sacred Feminine, this is the closest that we can come.'

'You too, James?' asked Emily.

The professor nodded. There was a moment of quiet understanding between the two of them before a door opened on the other side of the room and a smiling man appeared. He was silver-haired and soft-faced with a beaky nose, and he wore a pair of wire-framed glasses and a well-cut silver-grey suit. James knew him to be the man in the photo with his arm around Gordon Sanitaire. His name was Seamus-Johansson Jones.

'So there you are at last, Emily,' the man said, as if he had been expecting her.

CHAPTER FIFTY-SEVEN

His British-accented voice was as soft and as smooth as his angora wool socks.

Emily recoiled. 'Who are you?' she asked.

'I own this apartment, Emily. Surely it is I who should be asking you the exact same question? But since I already know who you are, allow me to introduce myself. My name is Seamus-Johansson Jones and you are Emily Raquin.'

Jones turned to Crack.

'James,' he said. 'I've been enjoying your work since we last met. You have developed a fine bland prose style even if you do put a comma after the word "and" all the time. It is popular and sells well and, at the end of the day, that is all that really matters.'

Crack shrugged modestly.

'James? How does he know you?' asked Emily.

'Oh,' said Jones, answering for Crack, 'James and I go

way back, don't we James? We used to be Jansenists, you know. Pre-destination and all that. Adolescent stuff, really, but there you are '

'And how do you know my name?' asked Emily.

'My dear, I know everything about you.'

Jones crossed to a mahogany Louise XVI writing bureau and opened it. Inside it had been converted to accommodate a 17-inch plasma flat screen, with a microphone and a joystick. He turned the screen on but received no signal. Emily and Crack realised at the same moment that Jones had been controlling Lord Wadley's every move from this eyrie. Now that Wadley was no more, the machine did not work.

'Such a shame. I loved that little fellow. I have no use for it now he's dead, but I monitored everything you did and said through this gizmo here.'

'Why?' asked Emily.

'Ah,' he smiled, turning to them. 'Of course. You don't know who I am. Will you tell her, James, or shall I?'

'Seamus-Johansson Jones is the head of the English Book Guild, Emily,' said Crack in a flat monotone. 'Also the head of the Uxbridge Road Group, too. He has been after the Asti Spumante Code for years. He is the one responsible for your nephew's death.'

'All true, I am afraid. I tried to reason with Sanitaire. I tried to offer him a deal. A huge advance. All the time in the world. I knew he had it in him, but he kept putting me off.'

'Had it in him? Had *what* in him?' asked Emily, bewildered now again.

'A book, my dear. In fact, not just a book, but *the* book. I wanted your nephew to write it for me, but he would not. Instead he kept writing delicate little stories about miserable Canadians.'

'Why did you kill him?' asked Crack brusquely.

'I wanted the Asti Spumante Code. He would not give it to me, I began to see that, but I knew that he would have to pass on the secret somehow and to someone. I was not sure that Emily here was the one. So I created Tod Wadley and let him loose on the world.'

Crack could not believe it. 'You created the most extraordinarily life-like robot, from which you could have made millions of pounds, and you're still a *publisher*?'

'I take your point, but imagine the power I will have when I possess the Asti Spumante Code. All I need to do is threaten a publisher and they will do exactly as I say. Soon there'll be no more of those excruciatingly sensitive slim novellas, no more coming-of-age-as-an-immigrant stories, no more narrative non-fiction, no more books set in Australia, nothing set at sea, nothing about gardening or circuses. Nothing narrated by a dog or a vase. Then anything quirky or amusing will go. All we will be left with are books about wizards, the Nazis, the Holy Grail and twenty-somethings who can't seem to land Mr Right or even Mr Wrong.'

Jones was over-excited now. A manic glint had come into his eye. He paced the soft carpet like a caged lion.

'What's to stop us calling the police?'

Jones held his hand to his ear and together they could just make out percussive thumps and wailing sirens as the men of SO13 finally mopped up the terrorists on the second floor.

'By the sound of things they're a bit busy, don't you think?'

'But,' started Emily, 'where is the Asti Spumante Code?'

Jones stopped and stared at her. He was about to say something when a buzzer sounded. He glanced at his Oyster Perpetual. Neither James nor Emily had moved.

'Hmph. Right on time. Rare in an author. Hold that thought, Emily. I will return to it in a minute.'

Jones swiftly crossed to a phone hanging on the wall and spoke a few words into it. The noise of an elevator whirring to life could be heard somewhere close by. Jones returned to sit by the piano. He tapped out the first few bars of 'If You Knew Susie Like I Know Susie'. He had a lovely falsetto voice.

He stopped after a moment and closed the piano lid.

'I thought that I'd found the Asti Spumante Code

somewhere else, you know. This author coming to see me now.'

A lift pinged to a halt and two doors at the far end of the salon opened to reveal a tall man in a dark tweed suit. He had sharp blue eyes, a strong clean-shaven jaw and dimpled chin. Grey highlights at his temples had recently made their way deeper into the thicket of black hair. He exuded scholarly allure and when he spoke his voice was like molten chocolate.

'Mr Jones? I'm Hubert Condom.'

CHAPTER FIFTY-EIGHT

'Mr Condom, good to meet you. Please, come in and sit down. In fact, why don't you all sit down? There is much we have to talk about.'

Jones made the introductions.

'Isn't it a bit late in the day to be introducing new characters?' Emily asked their host.

Jones merely smiled enigmatically. 'Oh, I think you'll find Hubert is a very old character, Emily. But your instincts are spot on, I must say.'

It was peculiar to hear Tod Wadley's voice pattern repeating itself and she nearly said something, until she remembered that to all intents and purposes, Jones *was* Wadley.

Meanwhile Hubert Condom had settled himself in one of the armchairs with his back to the hallway through which Emily and Crack had arrived. He put his leather briefcase on the coffee table before him and took out a thick manuscript bound in a plastic wallet, which he placed on his knees as if it were a cherished child. Emily, sitting on the divan next to James, estimated that it was at least a thousand pages. It might make a book about six hundred pages long, she thought, a real doorstopper.

It was the first time either Crack or Emily had sat down to rest since they had left the Range Rover earlier that morning. The professor was bitterly tired, but he yearned to know what was going to happen next. Where is the Asti Spumante Code? he could not help wondering. Did Emily really know where it was?

Meanwhile Jones was talking. 'Perhaps I should explain what we are all doing here. Hubert is here at my invitation to talk to me about a book we both feel shows some promise. Emily and James are here on something of a quest themselves.'

Emily could not get comfortable with the prolix in her sweater pocket digging into her belly. She pulled it out and placed it on the table next to Hubert Condom's briefcase.

Condom instantly leaned forward, his fine eyebrows knit in a question mark. He stretched a hand out to take the prolix, but withdrew it at the last moment, as if realising without it being spoken that the prolix was a thing of great value to Emily.

'Excuse me,' he said, 'can you tell me where you got that?'

Emily found herself blushing. 'My nephew left it to me, Monsieur Condom,' she said with a simple shrug of explanation.

Condom frowned and then reached for his brief-case. From within he pulled a similar looking object. He placed it next to the prolix. It was exactly the same. Another prolix.

'But how could this be?' said James Crack, leaning forward and studying the two books. 'Where did you get it?' he asked Condom.

'My aunt gave it to me. She said it would encourage me to write.'

And then from the front page, James Crack took an old black-and-white photograph that Emily instantly recognised. It was a picture of her with her twin brother.

'That is me and my sister,' said Condom. 'She was killed in a car crash when I was three.'

At that moment there was a crash of glass behind Condom and the sound of running feet. Suddenly a vile-looking albino in a black boiler-suit charged into the room, a samurai sword held high above his head. His eyes were the colour of blood and it was clear that he was insanely evil. He loomed up behind Condom and stared at them all for a second. Nobody moved. Then the albino brought the sword down and, with one horrifying sweep of its tempered blade, he removed Hubert Condom's head from his shoulders.

'Ah,' said Jones. 'Such a pity.'

CHAPTER FIFTY-NINE

James Crack woke from the most delicious three-day-long sleep he had ever had. The sun was streaming in through the windows of his hotel – the Holiday Inn in Bruxelles – and as he stretched his limbs languorously he wondered if he had been dreaming. And then it all came back to him.

Condom's death was to be deplored, of course. The man had so much to give, but as Seamus-Johansson Jones had said, he had taken his novel about as far as it could go. He was not the one with the gift. He was not the *Mûre-de-Paume*, the legendary keystone. That was Emily. In Condom's dying spasm he had hurled his manuscript across at his sister. It had landed in her lap, the right way up, facing her, its first page open. *Surely a sign?* thought Crack.

The albino that had killed him would never face trial now, thanks to the quick work of Lieutenant Dijon who

had been with Glover after the fire-fight had ended on
the second floor with the death of every single one of his
crack albinos. Glover had seen what had remained of his
men and the shock had driven him insane. Dijon had had
no choice. He had shot Glover in the back of the head
just as the Detective Inspector was about to attack
Seamus-Johansson Jones. He had saved a life, but at the
loss of another.

Foyles had been razed to the ground with the death of
every one of the insanely evil albinos and, regrettably,
Capitaine Taureau, who had become mixed up in the
fire-fight at a late stage.

Jones had been visibly shocked by the events, too. He
had, however, recovered immediately and offered Emily
a good six-figure advance for a two-book deal. The first
book would be an adaptation of Hubert Condom's
manuscript and the second would be based on the events
of the past night and day.

On his way back to Brussels Crack had sat with Emily
on the Eurostar, retracing their steps. He had stared out
of the window, dog-weary and absent-minded, while
across the table of the first-class saloon Emily had read
through her dead brother's manuscript. She had brought
all her bibliotechnigraphical skills to bear, correcting the
plot, refining and defining the characters, changing the
pace here and there, eradicating implausibilities and crass
Americanisms, tightening the dialogue and including her

own research. Towards the end of the two and a half hour journey she had finished the job. She hefted the manuscript onto the table, letting it shut. Crack leaned forward and peered at a scribble on the title page:

The Asti Spumanti Code.